Being a Vampire
Seattle Vampire Tales Book One

I'm still awake when Robert arrives. He scowls at me in the faint light, an angry scarlet glow touching his cheeks, then lies on the far mat. He doesn't blame me for the raid, does he? I hope he doesn't decide to take it out on me, like my eldest brother used to do. This entire group's dangerous, and not only to the people they bite. They're nearly as undisciplined and reckless as the one I stayed with in San Francisco in the early seventies. I ran out of money that time, too. When I escaped from them, I swore I'd never get into that situation again. And I didn't—until this year.

How long until I can get away from here? I was lucky tonight, already finishing work for the week before unexpectedly becoming unhoused—again. I can't afford to miss any work and lose my job, or I'll never live by myself. It's been far too long since I felt safe.

Praise for
Being a Vampire

Ramona Ridgewell breathes warmth and human life into vampire fiction and bends it to speculative fiction's highest purpose: using the imaginary as a lens to see reality more clearly than we could otherwise. We mortals may age and forget, but BEING A VAMPIRE captures the soul of a specific time and place—Seattle in 2020—and makes its memory immortal, enthralling, and sharp enough to break skin.

— ELLY BANGS

In this work of *vampirica literatura vérité*, Ridgewell explores vampirism as a slice-of-life lens on the cyclical societal pressures which impact marginalised communities and weave fear and violence into the fabric of survival. There is a constant balance in this work between the need to be part of a community, the peril of being caught in toxic circles, and the difficulties of trying to escape, knowing you may never break the cycle you are trapped in, but trying regardless because without the hope that there might be something better, eternal life just might not be all it's cracked up to be.

— DAN RABARTS

A deeply immersive tale and disturbingly realistic story of a vampire trying to create a safe, and moral, existence in the margins of contemporary Seattle. Coding gigs, coffee dates, rising rents and —blood.

— K.G. ANDERSON

BEING A VAMPIRE

SEATTLE VAMPIRE TALES
BOOK 1

RAMONA RIDGEWELL

Intrepid
Turtle Press

Being a Vampire
Seattle Vampire Tales Book One

First edition: October 2024
Intrepid Turtle Press
2442 Market St NW #393
Seattle, WA 98107

Cover illustration and design by Jamie Noble Frier (The Noble Artist)

Print ISBN-13: 979-8-9908723-0-1
eBook ISBN-13: 979-8-9908723-1-8
Library of Congress Control Number: 2024913060

NOTES TO READERS

Thanks so much for taking an interest in my story. It's filled with vampires eking out an existence in modern-day Seattle, beginning on the eve of the COVID-19 pandemic and barreling right on through its early days. The main character, a vampire named Rix, relates what he is observing—an impartial witness to a defining moment in history. But no one is immune from the impacts of the upheaval the pandemic brings.

This content is not intended for children or youth due to violence, sexual situations and other adult themes. Rated R.

Because of potentially triggering circumstances, I included content warnings at the scene level in the Footnotes, which can be found on my website: https://www. ramonaridgewell.com/footnotes-being-a-vampire.   The Footnotes also include links to real places and events referred to in the story.

Key content warnings and triggers include:

- vampire violence (of course)

- rape

- the COVID pandemic

- food, housing and employment insecurities

- abductions of vampires

RAINN is the National Sexual Assault Hotline: Confidential 24/7 Support. https://www.rainn.org/resources.

I wrote this story as the real-world events were unfolding, so many of the reactions, comments and incredulity were my own, just told via my characters. An example is the final scene in Volume 2: Vampire Heart, Chapter 3: Hungry, where Rix wanders through Ballard, noting the seas of unhoused folks lining the streets, as well as the murals that covered storefronts along Ballard Avenue. The scene was written as soon as I returned from my walk through Ballard that day.

I hope you enjoy the story.

NOTES ON AMERICAN SIGN LANGUAGE

For the American Sign Language (ASL) conversations in this novel, I used italicized text within double quotes for the dialog. I chose this convention for the convenience of the reader, since ASL does not directly translate into English.

I use the term Deaf to describe my deaf character. One usage of this spelling is to indicate someone who uses ASL as their first/primary/only language, generally due to being pre-lingually deaf.

For my mother, Mary, whose never-ending support of this endeavor lasted until the end. I wish I could have published while she was still living.

Vampire Jumprope Chant
  Vampire, vampire, in the night
  Don't let him close or he'll give you a bite
  Put him in a box and bury it well
  If you forget, you'll end up in ... (repeat ad finitum)
  - Ramona Ridgewell, 2024

VOLUME ONE: VAMPIRE EXISTENCE

1

SAFE PLACE

November 3 to 4, 2019
Rix

"Jeez, Rix," Robert hisses. He rolls away and pulls the blanket over his lank ash-brown mop of hair, dragging my power cable with it. "Could you type a little quieter?"

"At least, I'm working." I stifle my rancor, careful with the aggressiveness of my tone—like I did so often with my eldest brother when I was a small boy. If it's not enough, he'll ignore me, but pushing too hard could be dangerous. Robert can be very dangerous. I need to move beyond my reliance on him. And soon. "When are you going to pay me back for your half of the rent? I didn't have enough to cover it this month, and now we're behind."

"Find a way to make more money. You still owe me for letting you stay at the house."

I debate whether or not to argue with him, but go

ahead anyway. "I've more than paid you back when I paid all of the last three months' rent. If anything, you owe me."

"Keep paying them something," he mumbles, voice muted by the covers. "They can't evict us. Lemme sleep."

How will I ever live alone again if I can't save any money? That's likely Robert's plan—keep me dependent. After untangling the cord and plugging it back in, I check the time. Still half an hour until sunset. The short November days in Seattle make things a little easier.

Robert gives another jerk to the bedding, forcing me to grab my laptop before it's pulled along with the blanket. Sharing a tiny apartment—and a double bed—with him seemed like a workable plan. Now, I'm beginning to doubt it. I should have trusted my gut, but I was out of cash and he paid for the first month—the last of his contributions to rent. To save some money, it may be best to move back in with Jewel and the others at the place where Robert houses them, in exchange for their services—which Arnoldo never needed to require. Despite the noise, I would have my own bed, and maybe even my own room. But, I didn't fit in there. I've worked hard to avoid the necessity of prostituting myself. James isn't staying there, either. How's he doing? I should try to locate him. Maybe we could share a place. It would be safer than my current situation.

My phone hotspot is not so hot. This basement's pretty much a dead zone, so checking email's out of the question, and with no wifi, I can't work during the day. Coding examples from tutorials offline sometimes feels like a waste, but it fills the time when I can't sleep—which is often.

Even though hunger gnaws at my empty belly, as soon as the daylight fades, I dash the several blocks to the library. It's a modern, community-oriented space wedged into the dense housing a block off the bustle of Broadway. A desk is so much better than sitting on the bed, and the internet connection is solid. Several tickets vie for my attention. I pick the highest priority one and dive in, taking many wrong turns in the modified code before isolating the problem, like finding my way in a corn maze. It can be tedious, but is gratifying when I discover the cause.

All too soon, a scratchy voice on the PA system warns, "The library closes in five minutes."

Where'd the time go? Popping open my email, I look for a contract renewal. Still not there. My knee begins to bounce. If I lose this contract, I won't even have a bed to sit on.

A Sunday night crowd packs Lost Lake Cafe when I arrive, but in the back of the bar, I spot an empty booth. Barely looking up at the server, I order coffee and fries, then raise my eyes to watch him walk away. I haven't seen him before. He must be new. While finishing my second ticket, a critical one comes in. I close my ticket and check the time. My four hours are up in fifteen minutes, but that critical one's still not assigned. I have to take a peek.

Hoping to show some extra initiative, I text my lead.

Nalini. The Mu Cephei server's down. Looked into it, but out of hours. Shall I continue?

Please do. Thanks for offering. I can approve four extra hours for you.

That works.

That's an unexpected boon.

The next time I look up, only two other couples remain in the bar. My waiter comes to refill my coffee—for the third time. "You're working late."

"Mm-hm." I attempt a little smile. When he sets the carafe on the table, I catch sight of my fuzzy image reflected from the glass. Did he see it, too? I clear my throat to keep his focus on me, and broaden my smile.

He basks in my attention. "Done with these fries?" The flash of a crystal on a glittering silver chain draws my eyes to his neck. My knee twitches in anticipation. He reaches for the plate. "You hardly touched these."

"Guess I didn't want them after all." I'm so hungry I'm nauseous, but not for fries. They're just for the sake of appearances, a necessary waste of money. When I tear my eyes away, they brush over the carafe. I shift in my seat, rest my cheek against my palm and move my eyes to my screen. "Thanks for the coffee."

At half past three, I text Nalini.

A code change introduced a bug. I rolled it back. Amik fixed it. Helped him with tests and added a new script. In staging. Prisha's aware and monitoring. Should be solid.

Good work! Been meaning to ask. Interested in a contract renewal? Half-time again, for 8 weeks.

Perfect.

That'll buy me enough time to break free of Robert.

Paperwork forthcoming. TTFN

Glancing around, I catch the eye of my waiter—at the far end of the bar, chatting with the bartender—and mime writing to ask for my tab. He comes straight over and slides the bill toward me. "Here you go, doll."

"You can keep the change." I slip a twenty across the table and peer into his blue eyes. Teal eyeshadow glimmers around fresh mascara. That wasn't there before. I don't usually feed on someone I might so easily run into again, but I'm really hungry, and it's very late. I'm unlikely to find anyone else before the sun rises. Mustering a winning grin, I ask, "What's your name?"

"Lauren."

"I'm John. What time do you get off?"

"You're my last customer." Above a tired smile, a rosy blush radiates through his makeup.

"You should've told me. I wouldn't have kept you."

"You're worth the wait."

"May I walk you home?"

Our footsteps echo in the empty street as we stroll down Tenth toward Union. When we get to the luxury car showroom, Lauren pauses to gaze through the glass. "Oh, they're so pretty."

"Mm-hm. Beautiful." I glance up and down the street. No people. No approaching cars. When my hand touches his, our eyes meet. "Let's go over here." I guide him into a recess. "It's more private."

"OK." He wears the dreamy smile of all my victims. I'm beginning to like Lauren, and I shouldn't. I almost let him go, but my empty belly rumbles. It's a necessary evil, Rix, no different than wasting the fries.

Laying my palm on his cheek elicits a gasp. As my fingertips slide to his neck, where the external jugular brightly glows beneath the skin, my gut churns in rhythm with his pulsing blood. My fangs extrude. I plunge them into his neck, then pull out a little to let it flow. Molten liquid gushes against my tongue and down my throat, filling my stomach. Heat spreads to my extremities. I feel almost ... alive. I push that thought away. Carefully pressing deeper, I tap the internal jugular to increase the flow.

I pull away before I'm sated, before I take too much, and hold my hand over the gash. Reaching into my pocket, I tug out a wipe and rip open the package. After running it over my mouth and hand, I swab the blood from the nearly healed wound. "Are you all right?"

"Yeah." He blinks several times. "Must've fainted."

"Maybe low blood sugar?" Maybe I did take a little too much, but my queasy stomach has finally settled. "Let's get you home." I take his elbow. "You can look at pretty cars some other night."

After making sure Lauren is safely inside his building, I don't arrive back at the apartment—really just a room, and a small one at that—until well after five, but the long November night provides an ample buffer. That's strange. The door's ajar. Is it risky to enter? Nudging it open a little more, I squint into the darkness, tensed to dash away. I'm met with soft grunting.

"Robert?" I whisper.

"Go away," he snarls.

My shoulders relax. A little. Stepping inside, I push the door closed. I keep my voice neutral. "Where do you expect me to go?"

"Who's that?" A muffled alto voice—a woman? a youth?—comes from under the covers.

"Don't worry about him."

"I'm going to clean up." I stuff my pack into the cubby with my small stack of clothing and toiletries. "And then I'm going to sleep. Please find somewhere else to do that." The toe of my sock catches on the peeling lip of what's left of the linoleum flooring, nearly tripping me. I pull them both off and toss them into the cubby. The cold concrete saps the comfortable warmth I gained from feeding right through my bare feet.

Even with the bathroom door closed, I hear their sex. Brushing my teeth helps mask the sound, but the grunts and moans grow louder. My towel lies in a damp heap on the floor with Robert's. I hang it, then consider whether or not to shower. Robert still hasn't cleaned the stall. It *is* his turn. The slimy floor's getting dangerous. That seals my decision. I take off my shirt, check it for blood spatters, and wash at the tiny sink as best I can. Of course, it hasn't been cleaned, either. Back in the room, the unmistakable odor of semen fills the air. So, not a woman. At least, they're quiet. After tugging off my jeans, I tuck them and my shirt into my cubby and turn to the bed. "Move over."

Robert curls himself tighter against the other person. Are they a customer spending the day here? Or maybe a midday snack? That wasn't part of our agreement, although he's not abiding by any of it anyway. Did he transition them? I hope not, but wouldn't put it above Robert. He's been rebuilding the Capitol Hill gang. Several members, including James, fled last summer—where did they end up?—after Robert took over by throwing Arnoldo out the second story window into the midday sun. He didn't even have a chance to scream before his remains billowed in the bright light. Did it hurt? I'm glad I couldn't see him combust.

I lie facing away from Robert but need to press my back against his to not fall off the small bed, reminding me of sleeping with my brothers. He should know that three people won't fit in a double. With my knees hanging over the edge of the bare mattress—the bottom sheet's wadded up under him and his partner—and only my arm as a pillow, I can't sleep. I *really* need to find my own place.

November 10, 2019
Rix

As the sun sets, I change into the last of my clean clothing and stuff what I've been wearing for the past three days into my backpack with the rest of my dirty laundry and my computer. If I hurry, there should be time to do a load at the laundromat on Bellevue Avenue before they close.

Robert sits up and stretches. "Hey, wash these sheets." He pulls the covers off DB, the young man he recently turned into a playmate, or maybe another prostitute—who also hasn't paid any rent—and tries to untangle the sheet from the blanket. "They're starting to stink."

They do stink. Is he using the room to sell sex while I'm away? I wish he'd share some of that money with me. He claimed he wanted a more private place, but if he wants to use this as a brothel, I'd be better off sleeping on a couch somewhere.

Cool evening air blows in when I open the door. How far can I push him without risking an encounter with the sun? "You wash them. I barely get to use them."

As the door closes behind me, something hits it, making a loud bump. Through the door, Robert's muted voice calls, "Get back in here, you little freak." His diatribe fades as I leave the yard.

Half an hour later, I close the lid on the washer and retreat to a chair to review the new Python version. My phone's signal is inadequate to start the download, so I'll need to upgrade later, but that shouldn't impact anything at work. Now I'm stuck waiting for the laundry to finish.

I browse the internet on my phone—mostly impeachment evidence gathering. I don't usually follow the news, but I've got nothing else to do until everything's dry. Even on the tiny screen and through his heavy makeup, the mango glow of the President's lies comes through as he denies withholding military aid to Ukraine while trying unsuccessfully to force President Zelenskyy to announce an investigation into Joe Biden and to admit to interfering in the election. Ukraine has enough going on without this kind of distraction. That's enough national news. I check the weather instead. Continuing unseasonably warm and arid days. It's supposed to be sixty tomorrow—is that a record?—and dry as a bone. I can't complain, but the ongoing drought is worrisome.

When everything's neatly folded and stowed in my pack, I head back to our room. As I round the last corner, I halt. A big black van blocks the driveway. Two men—in riot gear?—guard the open rear door. Every instinct tells me to run. Trying desperately to control my panic, I retreat at a quick walk the way I came.

Before crossing the next intersection, I peek down the street. Stark naked, Robert dashes from between the apartment buildings directly behind the house where we're renting into Pepe's Garden across the street. My chest clenches. Two black-clad figures pursue him. He's fast. Much faster than ordinary men. Faster than most vampires. Maybe he can escape. Vampires can't afford encounters with the police. Getting arrested would likely be a death sentence. I don't want to suffer the same fate as Crystal, who was released from custody right after daybreak. She didn't have a chance to find refuge ahead of the sunrise. I need to get away from here.

Sticking to the shadows, I change course and wind my way over to Fifteenth. Those men didn't seem like cops, and I didn't see any markings to identify who they might be. What can this mean? Robert has never been very discreet. Did he put a target on our backs? And what do I do now? No shelter. No cash. Should I risk going to the house to warn the others? The evening's a balmy fifty, so lots of folks are out. A good night for hunting. Everyone's probably on the prowl by now. I'll look around the area, then head down to Seward Park. It'll take a couple of hours to walk there, but I know of several safe spots to hide during the day. I trudge along, searching for familiar faces, trying not to stick out too much. It may be time for leaving the Hill—or even Seattle.

November 10 to 11, 2019
Rix

When I reach the Safeway, I slow to blend in with the foot traffic. Outside the store, I spot James, who I haven't seen since last summer, with his arm draped around a woman. Her adoring gaze, and cheeks that shimmer in a pink glow reaching to the tips of her ears—a stark contrast to his ashy pallor—tell me she's not his victim. Just the opposite. Is he dating her?

"James," I call, moving toward them.

He stops to scan the crowd. His normally shaggy

brown hair is neatly coiffed. When I'm closer, he spots me, and his face glimmers a muted periwinkle. "Hey. It's been a while. How are you?" His friendly tone reassures me. I look from him to the woman. He squeezes her shoulder. "This is Darah. She's cool." He kisses her cheek. "This is R—"

"I'm John," I quickly interject before he shares my real name.

Her smile widens, warm and friendly. "Nice to meet you."

"The pleasure's mine."

"We're getting coffee. Wanna come?" James asks.

I glance around. "Sure." I'll be safer off the street.

James walks on the far side of Darah, arm still slung across her shoulders. She loops her arm around mine, pulling me close.

Stiffening, I force a weak smile. I hate being touched. "Um ... We're taking up the entire sidewalk."

"Yeah." She plants a quick peck on my cheek, lipsticked lips burning like tiny flames, then murmurs, "You're as cool as James." When she turns back to him, I rub the residue from my cheek.

At Starbucks, we huddle around a small table. After a quick sip of her coffee, Darah squeaks her chair away and stands. "I'll be right back."

I peek over my shoulder to ensure Darah's out of sight, then put my focus on James. "Please don't introduce me by my real name."

He looks chagrined, but angry red flames flicker around his face. "Aw, c'mon. What difference does it make?"

"It makes a difference to me." That was too loud. I lower my voice to a whisper. "I pay good money for my human credentials."

"OK. Sorry. You seem really stressed." James leans closer to study my face. "Well, more stressed than usual. What's going on?"

"I have no idea. I was out doing laundry, and when I got back ..." I shrug weakly. "It was a raid, but I don't know why."

"You mean cops?"

"Well, that's the strange part. They were dressed in riot gear. And there were a lot of them. They wouldn't do that if Robert was being busted for sex trafficking." Oh. Could they be targeting vampires? He prostitutes out all of the others to humans. Way too much exposure.

"You're sharing with Robert?" He swallows a laugh. "Is he using your place for that?"

"I don't think so." Is that true? "Maybe."

"Did they catch him?"

"Um." I cradle my forehead for a moment. "I just don't know. I saw him running away, naked." At this, James laughs aloud. I shake my head. "It's not funny."

He stifles his grin. "Robert's really fast. He probably escaped."

"There was someone else staying with us, too. I doubt he got away. They may be looking for me. I need to really lay low for a while." At Darah's approach, I lean back and take a sip of my coffee. She sits and scoots her chair into the tight space, so close her knee presses against mine.

"You working?" James asks me.

His casual change of subject gives me a moment to collect myself. "I found a remote DevOps contract."

"You nerd." He smirks. "Sounds more fun than washing floors and cleaning toilets, but at least I pay Darah some rent."

"You pay me in other ways." While she nuzzles his ear, her hand drops onto my thigh. I shift but have no room to evade her. She turns to me. "Where are you living?" Out on the street, a siren wails. A tremor in my gut races down my leg. I put my hand over Darah's. The jittering stops. Her large brown eyes fill with concern. "Baby, what happened?"

Flashing lights rivet me. A police car flies by, with a black van in its wake. "Um ..." I try unsuccessfully to relax the tightness in my chest that makes it impossible to inhale, let alone to speak.

"Come stay with us for a few days," James blurts, then shoots a glance at Darah. "That'd be all right, wouldn't it?"

Her smile returns, along with a lusty carnation glow. "We can squeeze in one more."

"If it's not an imposition." I look down at my coffee. Darah's fingers chassé up my thigh, but I stop them with gentle pressure from my hand. "Please don't."

"I'm not sure he's into women, Darah." James grins at me "Or threesomes."

I give him a scowl before turning to her. "It's just ..."

"That's OK." Her smile's genuine. "The sofa's comfy."

At seven, the barista shoos us out into the moonlit night. Darah squeezes between James and me, linking elbows with us. "It's too early to go home. Let's go to Sam's."

"Sure." James glances past her at me. "What do you think?"

"I don't really drink." And Sam's is too crowded and dark and noisy to work.

"Let's go talk at Lost Lake. They're open all night." Darah tugs on my arm. "My treat."

"Um." I'd rather not run into Lauren. It's too soon. I don't want to spur any memories of our walk.

"Come on." James grins. I've never known him to smile so freely. "Loosen up."

"Please?" Darah's face shimmers.

I guess it'll have to do. I don't want to walk away from a safe place to sleep. "OK."

As usual, the cafe's busy, but we get seated immediately near the rear. Even though I prefer to see the door, I sit facing the back, in case Lauren walks past. The escape through the kitchen door is visible.

After a lengthy wait, the frazzled server comes to take our order. "Sorry it took so long. I'm also helping in the bar. The other waiter didn't show." I hope that's not my fault. She tries to smile. "He said he's got a nasty flu." That's a relief, in a weird way. She fumbles around with her order pad, then asks, "What'll you have?"

"A margarita." Darah's tongue runs over her lips. "And we'll share some nachos."

"Margarita," James adds.

"Coffee. Black." I scoot into the corner. "Do you folks mind if I work?"

"If you must." Darah turns her attention to James.

The food arrives, followed by a second round of drinks. I hardly notice. When the waitperson comes to take the half-eaten remains of the nachos, I hurry to hand off my current ticket. Darah pays, and we head out.

After we cross Madison, the vibrant nightlife of the Pike Pine Triangle gives way to quiet, older neighborhoods. Darah's house is out past Union. As we duck through the gate, I take in the small, tidy yard. "This is nice, Darah. Where do you work?"

"Amazon." She unlocks the door. "But I grew up in this house ... when the neighborhood had a different kind of diversity. Come on in." As she shuts and locks it, she sighs. "Folks like me, but they're mostly gone." In the bright light of the foyer, behind the makeup that lightens her skin and reshapes her eyes, I notice the slight epicanthic folds of her eyelids. After clearing a few things from the couch, she fluffs the cushions. "James, go find a blanket and pillow." From a hallway closet, she pulls out bed linens.

I step out of her way. "How long have you known James?"

"Since last summer. I keep him warm at night." Giving me a sidelong glance, she smiles seductively. "I'd be happy to keep you warm, too."

"I'll be fine here." I move my focus to my phone. "It's past two. Do you always stay up this late?"

"Mostly." After tucking the last bit of sheet under the cushion, Darah nods at my pack. "Is that all of your things?"

"What's left. I only have them because I was out doing laundry when ..."

"When what?"

"I don't know." I shudder. "I didn't stick around when I saw my roommate running from some cops."

"It should be quieter here." She touches my shoulder. "Get some sleep. Things'll be brighter in the morning."

November 11, 2019
Rix

I run from my brother, Alan, but his legs are a lot longer than mine. He's getting closer. He grabs my shirt. We tumble to the ground. Why doesn't Mama stop him? Loud grinding jolts me awake, followed by the burbling of a coffeemaker. I open my eyes to a strange living room. Where am I? The sky outside the window blinds me, although the sun's not yet up. I'm normally careful about shades before I go to sleep. Yesterday's events come flooding back. The stress exhausted me more than I realized. I haven't slept soundly enough to dream in ages.

As I sit up and grub around for my clothing, Darah pokes her head from the kitchen doorway. "Good morning, handsome. Sorry I woke you." She's wearing my t-shirt. "Hope you don't mind that I put this on." Plucking at the shirt, she comes to sit on the coffee table. "I wasn't sure how you'd feel about me walking around naked."

I quickly gather the covers around my waist. "I have another one."

"Don't worry." Mischief tweaks her smile. "I'll give it back before I head to work."

"Veterans Day's a holiday." I'm a veteran. Is there anyone left to mourn for me?

"Not at Amazon."

"Are you still OK with me spending the day?" With all her flirting, I doubt she's changed her mind.

"I was planning on you being here when I get home." She leans forward, causing her black hair to drape in waves along her cheeks. When she puts her palm on my knee, I squirm. Her cheeks glow pink with lust. "Just make yourself comfortable. I'll be home by six." She works her hand under the blanket onto my thigh.

"Um." I pull my leg away. Sleeping without underwear is a mistake I won't make again, even if it means needing to wash them more often. "Is there a wifi I can use?"

She sits back, barely concealing an exasperated moue. "I'll write it on a pad in the kitchen. Do you want some coffee?"

"Please." I try to smile.

After she leaves, I tug on my boxers and jeans, then dash over to lower the blind. Before I have a chance to retrieve my clean shirt, she's back with two steaming cups. Setting one down, she sits and pats the couch. I join her and pick up the cup on the table. She scoots closer. A pale scar, barely visible on her neck, faintly glows a little brighter than the jugular that pulses just beneath it. Is that new? I drop my eyes to my cup. When she runs her fingers up my arm, I lean away.

"You're darker than James, but still look like you never get any sun." Her hand continues up my neck and lands on my cheek. "And you're just as cool." I stretch forward to set my cup down, breaking the contact. She sits back.

"You're going to be a challenge," she mutters, so soft I'm not sure I was meant to hear.

Turning sideways, I draw my knee across the cushion, as much to put distance between us as to see her better. "James and I sometimes depend on each other. I'd hate for anything to come between us."

She pouts. "Like me?"

"I'm not interested in a relationship. It has nothing to do with you."

"You've probably never met a woman like me before. I could take you places"—she leans closer, with her forearm on my knee—"you've never dreamed of."

"If you knew anything about James, you'd understand you're playing a dangerous game."

"Life is dangerous." She withdraws and stands. "It's part of the fun." Slipping off my shirt, she dangles it in front of me. I avert my eyes and grab it. Before it's over my head, she disappears through the door.

November 14, 2019
Rix

Midday, I awaken from another disturbing dream. Vague images of a battlefield, and broken bodies I can't fix, flitter away. Sleep is a mixed blessing. Even with the blinds down, my arm no longer adequately blocks the light. Darah and James were quite loud last night. How does she get by on so little sleep? Unless she sleeps at work?

After showering, I run my new comb through my hair, which feels way too long. I lost my scissors, left behind along with the rest of my toiletries at the apartment, so I can't cut it until I can afford a new pair. I could barely afford the comb, a toothbrush, toothpaste and a razor. I wrap a towel around my waist, and throw all my clothing into the washer. I have only enough to last four days, even rewearing some, and everything needs washing again. Have I already been here that long? While I wait, I reheat the dregs of the coffee. Burnt and bitter, it's too disgusting to drink.

By the time I dress and begin folding my things, James, wearing only bikini briefs, teeters blearily into the living room. "Why's it so bright?" Slumping into the chair across from me, he rests his forehead in his hands.

"The sun's still up. It'll be down soon." I fold the last shirt and start turning the cuffs down on matched pairs of socks. "You two were up late. Did Darah sleep at all?"

"She says she gets enough." He lifts his head, grinning sheepishly. "Did we keep you up?"

I nod. "Then, the sun woke me. But I got my laundry done." I set my stack of clothes aside. "James, what's your relationship with Darah?"

"You should join us." He smiles. "She'll make it fun."

"Is biting her part of it?"

His eyes drop. "She's into that."

"So, you're feeding on her"—I frown—"during sex?"

"It's kind of like choking. She sometimes asks me to feed until she gets lightheaded." He meets my gaze. "I think she wants to be a vampire."

"She has no idea what that means." That was louder

than I intended. My knee shakes. "Don't do that," I say softly, "please. Seattle doesn't need another vampire." The *world* doesn't need another vampire.

"I know, but ..."

"You haven't fed her any of your blood, have you?"

"No." He snorts. "I don't need a pet." He sucks in his lower lip. "She did ask. That's what the argument was about last night." The faint colors radiating from his face swirl from saffron concern to orange fear before landing on an embarrassed ruby. "Then, we made up. That was probably louder than the fight."

"Some people come to vampires to hang onto their youth before it slips away." My voice lowers to a hush. "They just don't know what they're asking for. Please James, be careful."

"I am," he says, a little too forcefully. The bright tangerine flash from his cheeks exposes his uncertainty. "How are you doing?"

"Still shook up about Robert and DB. Worried about Jewel and Dan and the rest. They don't do well on their own." The tremor in my knee turns to a bounce. I stifle it with pressure from my hand. "I swung by the house the other night. There was a red X taped to the window. Hopefully, everyone got out, and the warning kept the others away."

"Well, at least we're safe." He meets my eyes. "I'm really glad you're all right."

"Thanks." I stand. I need to get out of here for a while. Go for a walk. "I'm going to work at the library. I'll be late returning."

On the way outside, I stop in the kitchen, and find a

couple of pie pans. After rummaging through the compost container that sits in the corner of the sink, I retrieve some scraps of fat that Darah trimmed from her pork chop last night and the remains of a turkey sandwich, which I chop up and throw into one tin. I fill the other halfway with water, check the time—good, the sun's down—then carry them to the tiny backyard. Nothing remains on the plate I set out yesterday. A crow alights on the fence to watch me put out today's treats. He caws three times, head bobbing. It's amazing how fast they begin to trust you if you feed them. So much less complicated than people. I smile up at him, and my shoulders relax. I'll pick up everything tomorrow. I need to get to work, and the Central Library's half an hour away.

November 14 to 15, 2019
Rix

"Get out, James." Darah's voice carries from half a block away. "I'm sick of your flip-flopping."

As I turn into the yard, I call out softly, "Keep your voice down." A shoe flies past my head.

"*You* probably changed his mind." The next one hits my shoulder.

Kneeling on ground strewn with his shirts, jeans and underwear, James bawls, "Darah, please." When I touch his shoulder, he buries his face in his hands.

"Don't come any closer, John," Darah bellows, cheeks glowing like stoked coals. "You're not welcome either."

"May I please retrieve my things?" I keep my voice calm. My laptop's in my backpack—that's the most important thing—but it would be nice to have a change of clothes. Keeping a single set clean is challenging, and I can't afford to replace them until I get paid.

As I debate enthralling her—afraid it will trigger me into feeding—she disappears inside, then returns with my little stack of belongings. At first, I think she'll hurl them into the yard, but she sets them on the top step, returns inside and shuts the door. The porch light goes out. Maybe now, the police won't come.

I slip my things into my pack. As I pass James, he looks up at me with a tearstained face. "What'll I do now?"

"Make up with her?" I shrug. "But you'd better do it soon, or find something to carry your things in. I'm going to look for some of the others from the house. Maybe I'll see you wherever they ended up." I hate to abandon him. "Would you like me to wait for you?"

He looks between me and the front door. "I don't want to go back to them." Standing, he brushes himself off and heads to the porch. "I'm going to talk to Darah."

"Be careful, James." At the sidewalk, I look over my shoulder. "I really appreciate you asking me to stay. Let's keep in touch."

I need to find a safe place before sunup, but have no funds to rent a room. I head to the Pike Pine Triangle, ending up at Cal Anderson Park. Even at eleven-thirty, a small crowd stands at a chain-link fence, watching a bicycle polo game in the courtyard. I join the spectators. After catching a whiff of blood, I skirt the fringes into the alley between the park and Rock Box, where karaoke blaring from inside competes with the sounds of the game. The smell of blood grows stronger. Further along, tucked into a dark alcove partially hidden by dumpsters, a couple appears to be making out. I wait until one of them staggers drunkenly away.

While the other neatens herself, I approach. "You took too much, Jewel. Be more careful, or you'll get us all in trouble." Did it have to be Jewel? I guess I don't have time to be picky.

"Quit your bitchin'." She bats her long false lashes. "Where ya been hidin'?"

Using my thumb, I wipe a red smear from the corner of her mouth. A dusty rose blush illuminates the shadow of beard making its way through her heavy makeup. She still hasn't moved beyond her attraction to me. I've never done anything to encourage her, except be nice, I guess. Could it be that? I do seem to readily attract people. Maybe it's something about me. "Working a little, but I'm out of cash." My eyes dart around the alley. "I need a place to spend the day."

"I'm headin' back now. C'mon. We can make room for you."

Jewel leads me east several blocks to a run-down house with blue tarps on the roof, near the PSKS youth shelter. I heard they're closing by the end of the year. How many of those kids will end up in Robert's gang? At the bottom of a short exterior stair, the basement door scrapes on the concrete floor as Jewel opens it enough for us to slip inside. "Make sure you shut it all the way."

When it's closed, I squint around the narrow, littered hallway, barely making her out in the darkness—and I have really good night vision. Grabbing my sleeve, she leads me into a room. A small amount of light leaks past the peeling paint that shades the only window. It appears big enough to escape through. I make out three inflatable camping mats, the center one already occupied, lining a wall.

"We need to share." She goes to the third mat. Nodding at the sleeping person, she says, "That's Dan. You remember him, right?" The young man Jewel transitioned. I can't forgive her for that. He was barely more than a kid. But I understand how lonely she was. I still miss my daughter. I nod. She points to the mat closest to the door. "Robert sleeps over there. Always out til the last minute."

"Oh." So he's not dead. These folks depend on him, but he'll only increase their numbers.

"He lost all his cash, all his stuff, ev'rythin', in that police raid. Did ya hear about that? Glad he wasn't stayin' with us. I'm too old for that shit." She brushes off the mat, squeezes it. After making an attempt to add more air, she offers it to me. "I'm no good at this."

I wipe the mouthpiece with my shirt and try to remember how to fill my lungs when not speaking. Drawing in a deep—for me—breath, I force as much air into it as I can manage, then quickly screw closed the intake. I hold the mat out to her. "How's that?"

"Thanks. You always take good care of me." Her smile glows a muted amber with sincere fondness. She drops the mat to the floor, then eases herself to sitting on it. "Good job. Hey." Squinting, she tries to see my face. "Weren't you two stayin' together?"

"We were. I was out. After the raid, I went looking for you, but only found James. I'm glad you're OK. What happened at the place where you were staying?"

"Robert came straight there, butt naked." She snorts a laugh. "He was so mad. He found some clothes and told us we were leavin'. Only me and Dan were inside, about to head out for the night. I taped a red X in the window to warn the others. Just like that, we scurried over here. Had to leave most of our stuff behind." Her lips turn down, surrounded by a muddy green shimmer. "All my other wigs and most of my makeup. Gone."

"I'm sorry. Did the house get raided, too?"

"Not as far as I know." She presses her lips together, her grief over her losses quickly replaced by an angry vermillion flame. Shakes her head. "But Fernando, the guy who owns it, decided it's too risky rentin' to folks like us. Robert can't pay him, anyway." Her expression brightens along with a dusty carnation blush. Her hopeful attraction to me is baffling. I've told her since we first met that I'm not interested. "You gonna stay here for a while?"

"I need to find somewhere with power and internet, so I can keep my job." Down here, I can't even charge my phone, which barely has a signal anyway. I cross to the far wall. "I'll sleep over here."

"Nah." She drops to her side on the mat. "The sun'll getcha. Besides, this side's dry."

I lie pressed against Jewel's back with an arm across her waist to hold myself on the too-narrow mattress. As much as I dislike her for what she did to Dan, holding someone—anyone I'm not biting—stirs up feelings I haven't experienced in a long time. Using my backpack as a pillow, I try to nap. I'm certain Jewel's asleep, after draining that woman so much. Dan's as still as the dead. He probably also fed. One nice thing about vampires is they never keep you up with their snoring.

I'm still awake when Robert arrives. He scowls at me in the faint light, an angry scarlet glow touching his cheeks, then lies on the far mat. He doesn't blame me for the raid, does he? I hope he doesn't decide to take it out on me, like my eldest brother used to do. This entire group's dangerous, and not only to the people they bite. They're nearly as undisciplined and reckless as the one I stayed with in San Francisco in the early seventies. I ran out of money that time, too. When I escaped from them, I swore I'd never get into that situation again. And I didn't—until this year.

How long until I can get away from here? I was lucky tonight, already finishing work for the week before unexpectedly becoming unhoused—again. I can't afford to miss any work and lose my job, or I'll never live by myself. It's been far too long since I felt safe.

2

INTENTIONS

November 15 to 17, 2019
Rix

I'm outside the basement door when the rays of the sun fall below the southwestern horizon. After rushing over to the mailbox service, half a mile away, I find my check in my box. It's only sixteen hundred dollars—they take out twenty percent for taxes—but it'll hold me over for a while. On this contract, I'll get at least a couple more checks. If I can find a studio for less than a thousand a month, which is doubtful, I'll be able to pay rent for three or four months. It's a start.

I head north. After crossing the Lake Washington Ship Canal, I peer around as I walk, watchful of local vampires. A cheap motel on Aurora Avenue North is seventy-five a night, plus taxes and fees, but if I pay for a week, one night's free. My need for a few days respite, and to escape from Capitol Hill, overpowers my penurious grip on my cash. I slide five hundred-dollar bills across the counter, and in return get a pocket full of change and a room key.

"That's enough quarters to run two loads of laundry and get everything dry." His mouth smiles, but not his face. "No laundry after midnight."

"Thank you."

As soon as I'm in my room, I put the *Do Not Disturb* sign on the door and secure the lock, a deadbolt that appears brand new. The original lock in the doorknob is punched out, leaving a peephole which a wad of toilet paper plugs. I'm relieved to find a strong wifi signal. When my VPN connects, I login to work, pull a ticket and begin to relax. I close a third ticket and check the time. Oh. I've gone over my four hours for the day. After closing the lid, I unpack the rest of my things. Then, I take a long, hot shower.

Clean and warm, I slip between crisp, white sheets in the safe quiet of my own room. The stress and tension from the autumn chaos that cling to my muscles, like the yellow and brown fall leaves on a bigleaf maple, begin to let loose and drift away.

Two afternoons later, I struggle to pull myself from a bad dream. It must be a dream. My brothers died a century ago. Alan, the eldest, pins me to the ground. I try to squirm, to get away, but he's so much bigger than me. My other brother, Gareth, holds down my arms and grasps my head between his knees. Why is he helping? Now, I can't move at all. "You listen when I speak, you little freak," Alan barks. He raps his knuckle against my chest. Hard. He knows it won't show. A lesson from Father, before he left for the war. Where's Mama?

I jerk awake. I still can't move. Oh. The sheets are wrapped around my arms and legs. The desperate feeling stays with me. Did my fear of what Robert might do trigger this? Will James turn on me, like Gareth did? I need to get him away from Robert. Or maybe I should leave town, but I need more cash to do that. I'm trapped here, as much as I was with my brothers. A move to this new neighborhood may be enough to keep me safe.

I try to work for a while, but can't focus. My hunger drives me outside. The bright pink remains of the sunset make me squint as I head north toward Green Lake, spurring me to walk in the relative shade of the buildings that buffer Winslow Place from the traffic noise on Aurora. Overhead, a raucous band of crows rushes toward their evening roost, maybe up in the park. On a picnic bench outside a small office building lie the abandoned remains of someone's dinner. The white paper bag holds half an order of still-warm fries, and a scrap of bun, drenched in grease from the hamburger it once enveloped. I take it with me. It never hurts to befriend the neighborhood crows.

At Fiftieth, approaching sirens capture my attention. My entire body tenses, preparing to bolt. Calm down, Rix. They're not police sirens. Two firetrucks rush toward me, lights flashing and horns blaring, forcing me to cover my ears. I shake off the panic as their howls diminish, echoing in the tunnel that passes under the highway. After crossing the busy street, I pass through a parking lot and into the maze of trails in the wooded parkland of aptly-named Woodland Park. Sure enough, crows fill the air, swooping and calling to one another before settling into the trees. I stop at a picnic area to watch them, and begin to relax. When I dump the contents of the bag onto a table and caw to get their attention, one spies me and darts down to take a look. As I back away, he cautiously drops to the other end, eyes me suspiciously, then sidles toward the food. Several more of his mob join him. "Bon appétit, mes amis."

As I continue deeper into the park, the landscape transitions to grassy rolling hills. A few joggers and walkers hurry along the trails in the waning daylight. Near a pedestrian overpass that crosses the highway, I loiter in the shadows until a lone walker strides out onto the path, and fall in behind him. He stops and turns toward me. His pale face glimmers a soft lavender, similar in shade to the French herbs my mother grew, which she brewed into a tea to ease my anxiety. She always had some, too. I could use some of that tea. This man is not anxious and shows no concern for my presence.

Walking up to him, I smile. "A little cool tonight, isn't it?"

"Do I know you?"

"No." I take a step nearer and touch his cheek. "Let's go over here where it's more private."

Smiling dreamily, he allows me to lead him into the shrubs that line the highway. Cautious of an encounter with a neighborhood vampire, my eyes sweep the area around us. I only feed for a short time. After covering the wound with my hand, I swab everything clean with a sanitizing wipe. "Are you all right?"

"I ... I think so." He blinks at me. "Do I know you?"

"We haven't met." As I retrace our steps to the path, he follows. I pat his arm. "Take care out here. It's getting dark."

"You, too." He takes off down the trail.

By the time I return to the picnic bench, nothing remains of the fries. "Kuck, kuck," a crow coughs. He dives toward me, but pulls up before striking my head. The last blush of daylight glints from a mylar ribbon as it flutters to the ground in front of me. After stooping to pick it up, I scan the sky, but he's already disappeared into the darkness.

November 17, 2019

Rix

Ahead of me on the path, almost to the parking lot, a woman kneels beside someone. They're hard to make out in the soft light that filters through the trees from the streetlamp. At first, I think I'm interrupting a couple having sex right there on the trail, but then I see she moves in the steady rhythm of CPR. As I begin to turn away, she looks up. Her intriguing eyes, sparkling black jewels, draw me toward her. The maize glow of her cheeks expresses concern, but for the man on the ground, not because of me. I stop a few feet from them. What am I doing?

"Do you know CPR?" Her pumping punctuates the words. "Will you help me?"

"Um." Moving nearer, I kneel on the other side of the man. "I can do compressions." I take over, thankful with all the worry over communicable diseases that mouth-to-mouth is no longer required. I'm uncertain I could manage that much breath. In the distance, sirens howl like coyotes. Neighborhood dogs join the chorus. I know help is coming for the man, but my gut tightens regardless.

The woman picks up her phone from the ground beside her knee. "Still no response, but I've got someone here to help now." She watches me. "He seems to know what he's doing. Oh, I hear the sirens. I'll keep you posted." She sets the phone back down. "Are you doing all right?" I nod as I try to keep rhythm with the 'Staying Alive' playing in my head. Around her slight smile, her aura cools to a less-concerned soft ochre. "You're doing great. Sorry it's taking so long. The local station's out on a call or they'd be here already." Several choruses later, she puts her hand on my arm. I almost jerk away, but keep pumping. The warmth of her hand permeates the sleeve of my hoodie. I hope she doesn't notice the hole in the elbow. "Stop for a sec while I check for a pulse." When I sit back on my heels, she presses her fingers to the man's neck. Shakes her head. "Let me relieve you." As she pumps, her thick curls spill loose from whatever was reining them in. "Not again." She keeps pumping. "Not now."

I pull the crow's gift from my pocket. As I gather her hair, my fingers linger on her neck for a moment. Her life's blood gently pulses beneath the surface. I swallow the saliva that puddles in my mouth, and slip the ribbon around her dark tresses, securely tying it, all while she continues to pump without missing a beat. Good thing I just fed or letting her go would be more … difficult.

The sirens grow louder. When two firetrucks race into the parking lot, the wailing stops. An EMT dashes toward us from one of them. I hop to my feet and move out of his way, allowing him to kneel across from the woman. While he sets up the defibrillator, she keeps pumping. I can't hear their words over the sound of another approaching emergency vehicle, this time the Medic Unit.

When the paramedic rushes to the downed man, the woman grabs her phone and gets to her feet. With all the people, I'm surprised she spots me. Holding her phone to her ear, she comes to stand beside me. "They're here. I'll let you go. I hope he's OK, too. Thanks so much." She pockets the phone. I only notice this peripherally. The flashing lights mesmerize me. She touches my arm, making me start. "Are you all right?"

My head spins toward her. "I—" The world fades to only her face, and I lose myself in her eyes.

One of the firemen approaches, breaking her thrall. "They got a pulse. It's a good thing you were here and knew what to do."

"I'm a nurse." She glances at me with a little smile. "But I had some help. I'm so glad you folks arrived when you did."

"It's busy tonight, or the Number Nine would've been here even sooner. Thank you both. You two have a good night." By the time he heads back, the medics are loading the gurney into the ambulance.

The woman turns to me. "Thank you for stopping to help."

"You're welcome." I love looking into her eyes. "I'm Rix." Why did I say that? I never share my real name with breathing folks.

"I'm Maggie." She smiles again, her face carrying a soft carnation glow. Whoa. She's interested in me. "Will you walk me home? It's not far."

"Um." I really should go back to my room to work. "All right." My weak-voiced agreement is a surprise. What's going on with me? I follow her out to Fiftieth, where we head up the hill to the other side of Highway 99. Her voice enchants me, but I barely hear her words.

"The CPR'll have to do for my aerobic exercise today. I was just heading out when I ran across that man." She pants between the words as the hill steepens. "If it's busy in the ER tonight, I'll probably make up for it." Without breaking her stride, she unzips her jacket. As I gaze at her, I nod, although I'm only vaguely listening. I draw in a deep breath. She smells good, even her sweatiness. "Do you come to the park often?" Her voice, raised in a question, draws my focus.

"Um." My mind stumbles through what she was saying. "Sometimes?"

When we stop to wait for a light, she looks me over. "Are you sure you're OK? You seem a little rattled." When I only blink, she frowns. "He'll probably be all right. Did you know Seattle's one of the safest places to have a heart attack? We had the very first Medic One in the country. Half the people who live here know CPR."

"Oh." Noticing my mouth still hangs open, I bring my lips together. What *is* wrong with me?

"You did a really good job. Most laymen need some instruction, but you jumped right in."

The light changes, and we head down Fremont Avenue. I struggle to construct a coherent sentence. "I ... um ... have some medical training." My reaction to her is unsettling, to say the least. Normally, *I'm* the one who does the charming. "So, you're an ER Nurse?"

"Nurse Practitioner. The ER needed extra help tonight"—she shrugs—"so I signed up for a shift." As we approach Marketime Foods, the anchor of the small Upper Fremont commercial district, she slows. "It's not like I have a lot else going on." She frowns and looks away, as if she shared more than she should have. Stopping completely, she turns to me. "Hey, I need to grab something at the store. Thanks for walking with me." She seems to have as much trouble looking away as I do. "Let's have coffee tomorrow, and we can talk some more. Meet me at Lighthouse Roasters at five?"

"I'd like that." I'm not sure what's going on. A date? I break eye contact, since she hasn't, turn my back and walk away.

November 18, 2019
Rix

I don't sleep well. Every noise awakens me: a big truck rumbling past on the highway; the rattle of the house-keeping cart; the crows cawing outside. Each time, the first image in my mind is the woman I met last night or, more precisely, her amazing eyes. When I look into them, the world—and all its worries—just melts away.

A little after noon, I give up on getting any more sleep, and take a shower. I wish I had something other than an old, faded t-shirt to wear, but at least it's clean. What am I doing going on a date? I've never been on a date ... well, not in almost a hundred years. And I can't get involved with a breathing person. Will I be safe inside a coffeeshop? It may be crowded. But I told her I'd be there.

I read news headlines and a couple of stories. I don't usually pay attention to the news, but I don't want to sound like I live under a rock. Outside of pre-primary politicking and the impeachment hearings, the only news is the record-breaking cold back East and the continuing drought in the West. I guess I'll talk about weather.

When the sun sets, I hike over the pedestrian walkway that spans Aurora. Misty rain dampens everything, except under the trees where none of it reaches the sidewalks. As soon as it lets up, the streets are dry again. The coffee shop's only half a mile away, and I'm a little early, so I drop by Marketime to buy a package of peppermints. Even though I brushed my teeth, I worry about my vampire breath.

At Lighthouse, a rush-hour line reaches to the door. I

pause with my palm on the handle, suddenly reluctant to enter such a public place. What if someone notices me? A man approaches, sipping his fresh to-go coffee. We peer at each other through the mist-clouded glass. I open the door to let him exit, and edge inside, barely able to swing the door shut behind me.

The heavy aroma of coffee tumbling in a loud roaster at the rear saturates the warm, steamy air. I glance through the throng. Tightness clenches my stomach, reaching into my chest, shoulders and groin. She's not here. I'll wait outside to see if she comes. Pivoting, I reach for the door, the escape from this noisy, crowded place, but the space has filled with more customers. Nausea wells in my belly as bodies press me from all sides. Swinging my head back and forth, I try to find an opening where I can squeeze through without bodily contact.

When a cool gust of air ruffles her dark hair, the woman three people ahead of me in line turns. "Rix!" She waves. A brilliant smile competes with the brightness in her eyes. They draw me like a beacon. My muscles release. She makes her way back to me, somehow managing to stay a few inches from my chest. "You made it."

"Were you worried?" I return her smile, and the residual tension in my jaw flees. "I'd never turn down a cup of coffee. You're buying, right?"

"Sure." She giggles. "I'm buying. What're you drinking?"

"Tall Americano."

"A couple of seats opened up." She points with her chin. "Go snag them for us."

At a tiny table with one side pushed against a wall

covered with local art, and four chairs clustered around the other three sides, I ask the couple who huddles at one end, "Are these seats open?"

The woman barely glances at me. "All yours."

I sit and look around. At every table, and the stools at the bar, people are reading or conversing—mostly, conversing. Even the readers occasionally turn to the person next to them to chat. As people enter, the folks behind the bar greet them by name and ask if they'll have their usual. I understand why it's so crowded, and why Maggie suggested we meet here.

As my eyes return to the line, Maggie—back in her original position—reaches the front. I watch her until she sets the cups on the table and sits. With the tight squeeze, her knee bumps mine. I try unsuccessfully to move my leg to give her more room. "Sorry," I murmur. The pair at the other end scoot over, old wooden chair legs scraping on the floor. This is all so pleasant and ... mundane. I haven't done mundane in a while. When she's settled, we sip our beverages.

"Careful, it's hot." She smiles, upper lip pencil-mustached in white froth that offsets the rosy radiance in her cheeks. "How was your day?"

"I can't get 'Staying Alive' out of my head, but other-wise, OK."

"I use 'We Will Rock You.' I actually like that song."

"You were amazing last night." I take another sip from my cup. She turns unexpectedly demure, the glow of her cheeks intensifying, and won't meet my eyes. Even though she's dressed in a floral blouse, I ask, "Are you working tonight?"

"No." Looking up, she licks away the foam. "I worked all day. I usually save the extra shifts for the weekends, unless the ER's really short-handed. What do you do for a living?"

"DevOps." When she stares blankly, I add, "I keep computer servers up and running."

"Nice. Do you live around here?"

"Sort of." Was that too vague? I swirl my coffee. "I can't believe the weather back East."

"It's so surprising." She sips her latte. "They're setting record cold temperatures, and here we are with a dry and balmy fifty. My yard could sure use some rain."

"It may rain tonight."

"I hope the next time it rains, it *actually* rains. A good soaking."

"Right." I've liked the weather. Rain and cold limit my hunting.

When our cups are empty, she smiles. "This was really nice. We should do it again."

"Maggie, may ..." I get lost in her eyes.

She looks at me curiously. "That's what my Dad called me."

"Maggie May? Like the song?"

"Oh." Her face lights up. "You were going to ask me something. Nobody uses *may*. It's so old-fashioned. What is it?"

"Am I allowed to call you Maggie May?"

"That wasn't your question." She rests her chin in her palm and gazes at me with glimmering onyx eyes. "But yes, you are."

"May I treat you to coffee next week, Maggie May?"

Opening her phone, she hands it to me. "Put in your number so we can text."

November 18 to 19, 2019
Rix

Back in my room, I log in at work and scroll through the new tickets. Five minutes later, I still haven't opened one. Thoughts of Maggie tug at my concentration. Will she follow through with meeting me again? What are her intentions? What are mine? This is ridiculous. I can't get into a relationship. "C'mon, Rix, focus." Now, she has me talking to myself.

A new high priority ticket appears, on the Cephei cluster where I've been doing root/cause analysis. Once I dig in, I follow the maze of changes and land on one made by Amik, whose change caused that failure on Mu Cephei earlier this month. This one seems related.

Amik's new and still learning. I urge him to do the work this time, including figuring out the tests that would've caught the bug before he deployed his code. Four hours later, our final test pass finishes, all green.

"Thanks for showing me that, John." Although the video auto-adjusts the colors, his flaming cheeks cool and his smile turns genuine. "I guess you're not the enemy, after all."

"We're on the same team. You implement the details, and I ensure things run smoothly when we deploy the code. Don't hesitate to send questions my way."

"Maybe by next time you'll get your wifi fixed and show me your face." His impish grin makes me wonder about his age. "Thanks again."

The late-afternoon coffee did its job a little too well, leaving me wide awake, but I'm already over my hours for the day. I hand off to Prisha and log out. After peeking outside, the light drizzle convinces me not to go for a walk. "Here's your rain, Maggie," I mutter. My weather app says it won't last. I'll just try later. Skimming the headlines leaves me uneasy. I've watched regimes rise to power, and right now this country's headed in a precarious direction: distraction and deception; smoke and mirrors. The results of these same tactics surprised a lot of Americans at the beginning of World War Two. I did my part to aid the fight, enlisting as a field medic in the Army Medical Corp. Folks wondered why the German and Italian people allowed it to happen. But it was happening in our country, too. A lot like it is today. Why don't people learn? I load up my tutorial and focus on that instead.

The next night, I head to Capitol Hill. I need to start looking for a more permanent place. I trudge all the way to Darah's to see if James made up with her. Maybe she'll let me crash on the couch again. When I knock, shuffled feet approach the door, but no one answers.

As I turn away, Darah opens it enough to talk. "James isn't here."

"Do you know where he's staying?"

"Not far. Around Nineteenth and Madison." She opens the door a little farther. "Where've you been?"

"Up in Wallingford. I just wanted to check in on James."

"If you find him, tell him I miss him."

"Sure thing." I start down the steps. "See you around."

Ten minutes later, I lightly rap on the basement door of the house where Jewel took me, then push it open and make my way to the dark room where we slept. A fourth mat lies squeezed among the others along the south wall. The lone person, lying on the farthest one, spins to a crouch. "Who's there?"

"James?"

"Rix?" He gets to his feet. "What are you doing here?"

"Looking for you."

"How'd you find me?"

"I asked Darah. She said she misses you."

"I'm done with her." He sits on his mat and pats next to him. "Have a seat. Tell me what you've been up to."

As he tugs his ratty shoes over dingy threadbare socks, I crouch. "I'm staying in Wallingford for a few days, but I'm looking for permanent housing. I could use someone to help pay rent. Are you still working?"

"Yeah. What time is it?"

"Almost seven."

"Oh, shit." Grabbing his pack, he jerks out a wrinkled shirt. "I'm late."

I stand and pull him up. "How much rent can you afford?"

"My take-home's just over six-hundred a month after Robert takes his share. How much would I need?"

"Let's see what I can dig up." As he rushes down Pine, his longer legs force me to jog to stay beside him. "It'll be hard finding anything on the Hill for less than nine hundred, even sharing a single room."

"It won't leave a lot." He waits for me to catch up. "But I'd feel safer rooming with you."

"Do you have a phone yet?"

"Can't afford one." He stops. "This is where you can find me, seven-thirty to ten, Monday through Friday."

"All right. I'll check back when I figure something out." Going hunting crosses my mind, but I want to get back to the room to work while I still have it. Besides, I just fed two nights ago, so why risk running into Robert.

November 19, 2019
Maggie

As I review notes for my next patient visit, I find myself staring at the screen, thinking about that guy—Rix—who I had coffee with last night. Is he my type? Do I *have* a type? I haven't dated enough men to even know. He does keep himself fit, if a little thin, but that's all right. It's nice that he's only slightly taller than me. No need to crane my neck to look up at him. I like his dreamy brown eyes and thick, wavy walnut hair. He could use some time in the sun, though, to add some warmth to his oddly pale olive complexion. Even though he appears to be around my age, he carries an old spirit. He seems genuine and kind, but something else about him intrigues me that I can't put my finger on. My reminder chimes, and I dive back into the patient's history, finishing just before my assistant pings me that he's ready.

When I return to my office, I check my messages and find one from Althea.

> Sorry for the late notice, but I'm short-staffed again tonight. Is it possible for you to come in for half a shift? 6 to midnight?

I take a quick glance through my calendar. Tomorrow morning's free.

> Sure. I'll head over as soon as I finish here.

> I knew I could count on you. :-)

The afternoon flies by and before I know it, I'm in the ER, donning my scrubs. As I head down the corridor in search of Althea, a familiar voice calls out, "Maggie."

From the approaching group, I pick out the compact man with warm brown skin, dark eyes and a bright smile. "Hi, Rama. I didn't know you were working tonight."

"Althea is a few people short, so she asked me to stay for an extra half shift." He walks alongside me. "I'm glad to see you. I'll try to sync up our schedules so we can eat together."

"I'll look for you. I came straight from the office, so I should have something."

He veers off at the next corner and I don't see him again until he pops up beside me just before nine. "Hungry?"

"Yes. I'll let them know."

"I already did. Let's go."

In the cafeteria, we find a private table and sit across from each other. He digs into his chicken breast as I nibble at my salad. Between bites, he sets down his fork. "You're quiet tonight. Is everything all right?"

"I had the most amazing experience Sunday night. I was out for a run and this man dropped to the trail right in front of me. Heart attack. I'm so glad I was there."

"Did he survive?" He takes another bite.

"I think so, even though the aid car took forever to arrive."

"In situations like that, time gets warped."

"Well, the local was out on a call, so they had to send one from another firehouse. I'm not sure I would've had the stamina to continue until they got there." When he leans closer, I smile. "But then, a knight in shining armor appeared."

"You had help?"

I nod. "We traded off until the medics arrived. He knew what he was doing. We made a good team. It felt great when they got a steady heartbeat."

"Did you get his name?" His brown eyes twinkle.

I can't hide my grin. "We had coffee last evening."

"Are you seeing him again?"

My teeth catch my lower lip. "Hmm. I haven't decided yet."

"Fair enough. Was there something that made you uneasy?"

I shake my head. "Just the opposite, really."

He raises his brows, waiting for me to continue. When I don't, his eyes pinch at the corners. "Then what's the holdup?" He shovels his remaining veggies onto his fork and pops them into his mouth.

"Me. I'm afraid. He seems too nice to be real."

Wiping his mouth, he studies me. "Perhaps you just need more information. And you won't find that if you don't see him again."

"Don't play matchmaker." I eat a few more bites of salad before rising. "We should get back to work."

November 20, 2019
Rix

Behind a large tree on one of the side trails near the Green Lake dog park, I run my hand down a jogger's neck to wipe away the sweat. Still panting from his run, his blood races under my fingertips. As I move closer, so close my fangs nearly touch his neck, a hand lands on my shoulder. I freeze.

"What's going on?" A woman? How did I miss her approach? I risk a peek over my shoulder. The minimal body heat signature confirms she's a vampire—as tall as me, and better fed. Arm muscles ripple under her teal athletic jacket. Her obviously bleached hair has buzzed sides, but the top, tipped with magenta vibrant even in this light, stands straight up at least two inches.

Another even larger vampire hulks behind her. With his dark complexion and clothing as black as mine, I struggle to make him out in the shadows. "Jutht having a thnack." A fang catches my lower lip, causing a tiny trickle of blood. Until they recede, enunciating without lisping is nearly impossible.

"You're new here." As she scans my face, I nod. She peers over my shoulder at my victim. "Who said you could hunt in these woods?"

I let him go. "You should be on your way." As he trots off, I turn to the woman. "I thought this was a public park." As preposterous as my statement sounds, I try to keep my voice confident, but not too aggressive.

"Why'd you let him go?" The heat emanating from the bare skin of her neck increases, rising to give her cheeks a faint glow. I hope she can't read me as easily.

"I didn't know your intentions."

When I glance at the other vampire, his shadow remains a cool, milky blue. Smiling faintly, he places his hand on the woman's shoulder. "Bry."

"I intended to feed." Her words sound rancorous, but the heat dissipates from her face as quickly as it arose.

The tension leaves my shoulders. "So did I." I smile. "I'm Rix."

Shaking her head, she snorts a laugh. "You're kinda ballsy. I like that. I'm Bryer." She thumbs over her shoulder. "That's Cleve. You planning to stay?"

"If that's all right with you. I'm checking out new neighborhoods. Tired of Robert's band up on Capitol Hill."

"They're a rough lot." Her eyes glint like moonlight on polished steel. "We never kill our victims. *Never.* We don't have trouble with the cops, and I want to keep it that way."

"I'm very careful." I hold my palms facing her. "It's one of the reasons I want off the Hill."

"You seem like a nice enough guy. You'll fit in down here. Come find me if you decide to stay. Good hunting." She slaps my arm, then turns to Cleve. "Let's go. We've got hunting to do."

When they're gone, I slump against the tree. I hate first encounters with vampires. They're unpredictable. Even these two. Bryer and Cleve. At least I have names now, in case I run into any others.

On the way up toward 99, I lure a woman off the trail. She's smaller than I thought, so I'm not satisfied when I let her go, but I don't have time to hunt anymore tonight. I should already be working. I can't afford to get fired.

As I near the exit, a woman trots onto the trail. Maybe I do have time for another nibble. Oh. It's Maggie. When she spots me, her face blossoms in a rosy pink glow. I wipe my hand over my mouth and chin to remove any lingering blood, and shoot a glance at my shirt.

She stops, panting, not three feet away. "I didn't expect to see you."

When I breathe in to speak, her scent intoxicates me. "Maggie." I slip my tongue over my teeth, ensuring the fangs have not returned. "I was just out for a walk. Are you safe alone in the woods this late?"

"I've lived in cities my entire life. I know how to pay attention." She points to her ears. "No earbuds. Stay on the main trails. Keep my eyes open." Reaching a hand to her waist, she pats a small cylinder. "And I've got mace, as a backup."

"Be extra careful tonight. I saw some ruffians harassing joggers down by the dog run." I can't warn her more than that, not without giving myself away. Much as

I'd like to, I can't stay. I'm already late for work. "Have a good run."

"See you soon." She dashes down the trail.

"Stay safe." I take an involuntary step to follow, but she disappears behind the trees. As I walk back to the motel, I can't get her out of my mind. My encounter with Bryer gives me a little comfort. At least, if Maggie does fall victim to one of the Green Lake community, she's very likely to survive.

November 21 to 22, 2019
Rix

At eleven, I'm up and dressed. How did it get to be Thursday already? I still need to find some rental rooms to check out, do laundry and be out of here, as well as find somewhere to spend the day—with James, if I can track him down—well before sunrise tomorrow. I don't relish returning to the Hill. I feel so much calmer since I've been away.

For a bedroom in a house with a shared bath, at eight or nine hundred, even without considering the damage deposit and last month's rent, I barely have enough. I'll be broke again until the end of next week. And I promised Maggie I'd buy her coffee on Monday. If she decides to ping me.

On the street that faces Interstate 5 in Wallingford, a basement room for eight-twenty-five sounds promising. If I had more cash up front, a longer job history and references—and no roommate—I could rent an aPodment for that price. In the email, I explain I can pay the first month now, and the second month in another week along with the four hundred for the damage deposit. And that there are two of us, which may be a deal breaker, but I'd like to help James get free from Robert. Plus, I can save whatever money he provides.

In four hours of looking, I send only five additional emails. The rest are even more than the first. I carefully note them, with their prices and locations, in a small note-book. A little old-fashioned, which is what Maggie said about my speech. I don't know if that's a good thing or not —I work hard to keep my vocabulary and tech skills current, so I don't stick out. My swirling doodles along the edge of the page turn into long, wavy locks, then a jawline emerges. And a neck. I close the notebook.

Going through my clothing, I look for holes. And stains. Blood's difficult to remove, so I avoid getting any on me, mostly successfully, but I check for it regularly. I don't find anything egregious, blood-wise. An armpit on a faded navy tee has worn through, and that's tough to do anything about with a needle and thread. And the elbow on my hoodie is beyond repair. Running over to the U-District to find a newer shirt or two, and maybe a hoodie, at the Goodwill or one of the other thrift shops in the same block just became a prerequisite to doing laundry.

When I examine the black t-shirt I'm wearing, the best one I own, I find a small hole near where it tucks into my jeans. I slide it off and zip open the front pocket on my backpack. After threading a needle with the last of the black thread in my tiny sewing kit, I darn the hole. Barely enough. I add black thread to my ever-growing list of needs.

At four twenty-six, I'm out the door with my empty backpack. The Goodwill is two miles away and closes at six, so I need to hurry. The t-shirts and hoodie will be cheaper there. A couple of the other shops don't close until eight. I also want a button-down shirt, for the next time I see Maggie, and they'll have a better selection.

I return to the motel with two lightly-used t-shirts and the zippered hoodie I've been wanting—all with the pink color-of-the-week price tag, giving me fifty percent off; I wouldn't have indulged in the hoodie otherwise—plus a nice black shirt. After throwing all of the clothing I own, except for the pair of jeans and worn out t-shirt I'm wearing, into the laundry, I get to work. It's nearly nine. Perfect. I have enough time to put in around four hours, with breaks to fold clothing and pack.

At one-forty, I slip on my bulging backpack—I had to discard the worn out hoodie and t-shirt to compel the zipper to close—and pull shut the door to the room. It's a half mile walk to catch the 5, scheduled to arrive at two-oh-three at the Aurora onramp. My only other option is to go north about the same distance to catch the E Line at two-oh-eight. Neither bus runs again for two hours. I don't understand Metro's propensity for scheduling buses that basically service the same area at the same time. But it's way faster than walking.

Boarding the bus, I fumble in my pocket for fare. I know exactly how much I have, and I'm a little short. While I try to smooth a very crumpled dollar bill enough to get the toll-box to accept it, the driver grows impatient.

She waves me past, already underway before I sit in the second row with my pack taking up the space next to me. Three more riders sit in scattered seats between me and the back row, where one's tucked into the corner, obviously sleeping.

"Next time"—the driver amplifies her voice enough so I can hear her—"don't pay with your last dollar." She meets my eyes in the mirror. "Just tell the driver you can't pay."

I nod my thanks. My phone buzzes. The message is from a number I don't recognize and tempts me with partial text: *Monday, same place, same...* I thumb it open.

> Monday, same place, same time?

An unfamiliar feeling ripples through my gut. Monday's fine, but I can't possibly make it to Fremont by five if I'm still staying on the Hill. Six may even be pushing it.

> Would 6:30 work?

> Not Monday. Tuesday? But they close at 7. Can you make it by 6?

> That could work.

But only if I'm lucky timing the 5.

> You're up late.

> Couldn't sleep. You are, too.

Just finished work. Hoping to sleep soon. What's keeping you awake?

The impeachment.

Whoa. I don't want to talk politics.

All we can do is pay attention and hope our checks and balances do what they're meant to do. Even if the guy at the top doesn't have a good moral compass, members of the Senate probably do. Not worth losing sleep over.

At least, not yet.

Also realized Thursday's Thanksgiving. Missing my Dad. :'-(

Holidays are rough. Sorry you're going through that.

A faint memory of a Thanksgiving flitters through my mind, with candles softly lighting a table set with a roasted chicken, sweet potatoes, stuffing and gravy. My daughter, Erianna, my sweet Eri, must've been five or six, in a frilly dress with her mother's long curls—like Maggie's, I realize, although not ebony, but dark walnut, like mine—falling in ringlets from where my wife tied them up with a ribbon. I close my eyes to push the image away, and blink away tears. The vibration of my phone draws me back to the conversation.

You're missing someone, too.

How'd she intuit that?

> It was a long time ago.

I glance outside. Oh, no. We already passed Stewart Street. I jerk the stop cord. Shouldering my pack, I stand as the bus comes to a stop at Pike.

"Be careful out there." The driver gives me a smile. "Have a nice night."

"Thanks. You, too."

Third Avenue's completely deserted. To put my entire focus on the streets around me, I pocket my phone. Pike Street can be rough late at night. I don't want to look like a tourist, and I certainly don't want to give the police any reason to stop me. Half a mile separates me from where I hope to find James, and a place to crash during the day.

My phone vibrates twice before I get to the other side of Interstate 5, but I don't pull it out until I cross Minor, where the Capitol Hill neighborhood starts. Except for the inherent danger of a vampire existence, I always feel safe on the Hill. After thumbing open my phone, I find an email from one of the places I contacted about a room, but the two texts from Maggie are where my eyes, and my thumb, land.

> I guess we all have our stories.

She posted this as I exited the bus. The next one came just a few moments ago.

> Are you OK? Where'd you go?

Had to step away. Sorry to cause you concern.

As long as you're OK. :-) There you go again with your interesting speech patterns. Where'd you go to school?

On the east coast.

I re-read my text. Should I have written, "*Sorry to make you worry?*" It's not so much where I went to school as when.

Are you sleepy yet?

Nearly dozed off waiting for your reply. Thanks for the chat.

See you Tuesday. Sleep well.

Several long blocks later, I push open the basement door of the house with the blue-tarped roof. The bottom scraping on the floor echoes in the quiet corridor. After feeling my way down the hall, I peek into the dark room. The closest mattress is empty. I can't make out the person on the next one, probably Dan, but I'm certain Jewel lies between them and whomever's at the end. Inching my way inside, I squint into the shadowy corner. Good. It's James.

"Jewel," I whisper. I don't relish startling a vampire awake, let alone three, and Jewel is the lightest sleeper, and the least jumpy.

"Robert?" she mutters, half awake.

"No. Rix."

She props herself on her elbow. "You need a bed today, lover?"

"Wake up James for me."

Rolling toward him, she cautiously touches his shoulder. "James, wake up."

He jerks bolt upright to sitting and peers around. "Oh, it's you," he mumbles. "What's going on?"

"Rix is here to see you."

He finds my legs in the near darkness and follows them up my body to my face. "What do you need?"

"May I share your mattress?"

Patting next to him, he scoots to the edge nearest Jewel and lies facing her. "Wake me in the afternoon."

"What's wrong with me?" Jewel whines.

"James is farther from Robert." I stow my pack in the corner.

"Scoot closer." James grabs the edge of her mat and tugs. "We'll all sleep together."

Lying with my stomach against James, trying not to press my back to the cold concrete wall, I close my eyes.

3

PROMISING

November 22, 2019
Rix

A screechy echoing grind startles me awake. What is this dark place? Am I back in that awful cell? I sniff. Oh. I'm snugged against James. Dawn's first light makes its way into the room. Must be around six-thirty. Neither James nor Jewel stirs. On the next mattress, the man rolls to face me but doesn't awaken. It *is* Dan. Shuffled footsteps draw my eyes to the doorway. A moan is followed by soft grunting. Easing myself up, I inch to where I can see down the hallway, lit from outside through the open door.

A man stands with his back to the wall. In front of him, Robert kneels. The man moans louder. When fingers brush my shoulder, I start, then turn to find Jewel peering around me. We move away from the door.

"Does he do this often?" I whisper.

"It's how we're makin' money to get outta here." She shrugs. "It's hard payin' the rent without beds."

The noise from the hallway increases steadily as the man reaches climax. James sits up and squints at us. I take another peek down the hall.

Wiping his mouth on his sleeve, Robert rolls back onto his feet and rises. The man buttons his jeans and tugs up the zipper. "You're so good, Bobby." He cups his cheek. "No one makes me feel like you do. I don't know how to repay you."

"Just pay up." Robert takes folded bills from the man, then guides him to the door and touches his cheek. "Go home and forget we came here, but remember how good it felt." He counts out the wad of bills, then shoves the door closed with a loud squeal. Before he makes his way into the room, I'm wedged between the wall and James, who feigns sleep. Jewel lies facing us with her eyes open. Will they side with me, or with Robert, if it comes to blows? He frowns when he sees me. "What're you doing here?"

"Trying to sleep. And you're keeping me awake, as usual."

"Asshole," he hisses as he kicks off his shoes. A flame flickers to life in his cheeks. "I didn't invite you."

I sit up, to be better positioned if he decides to attack, and keep my voice steady and calm. "I need a place for the day. If you pay back what you owe me, I'll go stay in a hotel. Otherwise, I'm sleeping here."

"Well, I'm letting you stay, so let's call it even." He lies on his mat, facing the other wall. "Go fuck yourself," he mutters. "I don't know why I put up with you."

Getting up, I walk down the hallway to explore the basement. When I return, I squat next to him. "Robert," I whisper.

"Go away."

"What happened to DB?"

He rolls to sitting. "He's gone." The smoldering coals die away. I can barely make out his features.

"Gone where?"

"I dunno. I never saw him again after ... that night." In the dim light, he looks sad, but exudes no aura. He's often difficult to read. He drops to the mattress. "Let me sleep."

I squeeze past James. Using my pack as a backrest, I sit with my legs along the wall. With my phone's light dimmed to its lowest setting, I open my email and scroll to the message about the room.

Dear John,

If you're interested in a short-term rental for a couple of months, I'd like to meet you and your partner. What time works for you? I can arrange most times tomorrow (Friday) evening until 9.

Warmly,

Silvan

This is promising. I nudge James. "You awake?" I whisper softly. He turns his head to look up at me. I position the phone so he can read it. Mouthing five-thirty, I hold up five fingers followed by three fingers, and wait for his nod.

Dear Silvan,

That's great news. James starts work at 7:30 on Capitol Hill, so we need to come around 5:30. Will that work for you?

Cheers.

John

After sending the reply, I open the text app and click Maggie's phone number to add to my contacts. Then, I re-read her messages and put a reminder in my calendar for our coffee date. The battery shows less than half, so I power down. Still leaning against my backpack, I close my eyes. I don't trust Robert, so try not to let myself sleep. Rustling draws me fully awake. Dan and Jewel sign a silent conversation. Beside me, James twitches in his slumber, like a cat whose paws move in pursuit of some dreamed prey.

"*I hate it here,*" Dan signs, I think. My ASL's not that great. "*I want to stay somewhere else.*"

"*I know, baby.*" Jewel brushes his unkempt hair from his cheek. "*We have nowhere else.*" She transitioned Dan to replace her own son, who was also Deaf. I'm surprised he's survived as a vampire.

"*Where we were staying was nice.*" His signing is silent. No vocalizations, no tap of hands coming together. I guess Jewel's persistence paid off. Absolute quiet is a vampire survival skill.

"*Robert has no cash.*" Her hands fly. "*He cannot even pay our percentages. Without his friend upstairs, we would not have this place."*

To give them privacy, I close my eyes. They spring open when James stirs and gets up to stretch his legs. Jewel and Dan sit against the wall passing a notebook back and forth, playing a game with dots and lines. I check my phone. Two-thirty. Two more hours until I can get out of this basement. I turn it off. James returns and lies down again. He peers up at me before closing his eyes.

At four-fifteen, I touch his shoulder. Everyone else is asleep. Groggily rubbing his eyes, he sits up. We quietly collect our things.

As soon as my phone's clock says four twenty-six, we step out into the November evening, unseasonably warm and arid. I'm glad for it, but remember Maggie's wish for a good soaking rain.

"Where is this place?" James switches his duffel bag to his other hand. "Is it far?"

"Over near the U-District. We'll need to take the bus. I'll pay for it. Be sure to get a transfer."

November 22, 2019
Rix

We take the 43 bus through Montlake, which skirts the UW campus, where it magically turns into the 44. The house is a short walk from the stop, back two corners on Forty-fifth and up Fifth a couple of blocks. Like a lot of the houses that face the freeway, it needs a little maintenance, but as long as the basement's dry, I won't complain. I buzz at the front door, and we wait.

A small, wiry woman—with skin the color of the ivory keys on the piano I played as a child, and neatly trimmed slate grey hair—answers. "Ah, John." She looks at James. People always assume the larger man is in control.

"I'm John." I offer my hand and wait while she eyes me before taking it. That contact should be enough for her to trust me. "You must be Silvan."

After we shake, she grabs a coat and comes onto the porch. "The entrance is around here." She guides us through a door a couple of steps down from yard level. "This is the shared laundry." She keeps walking down the hallway and points to the opposite side. "And the bathroom. Towel racks and cabinets for your toiletries are in the laundry room." A door opens and a bleached-blonde head pokes out. "Clarissa, this is John and James. They may be taking the vacant room until next term starts."

Her bright green eyes dart over us. "Oh. Hi." She closes her door.

"And here"—Silvan swings open a door and turns on the light—"is your room."

A double bed takes up most of the space. A desk and a small upholstered chair occupy another corner. Random Ikea shelves and cubbies line one wall. I'm fairly certain the window faces north. "When can we move in?"

"Just so we're clear: no smoking; no drugs; no loud music. I usually only rent to serious grad students but one dropped out, so her room became available." With raised brows, she focuses a steely gaze on me until I nod. "Let's take care of some paperwork, and then you're set." On the desk, Silvan lays out a rental agreement. I glance at it and pull eight hundred-dollar bills, a twenty and a five from my pocket, stacking them next to the document. James stares at the cash. "You both need to sign." She offers me a pen. When I'm done, James looks from the little pile to me, then takes the pen. After he signs, she scoops up the money and the paperwork, and drops some keys on the desk. "Here's two exterior keys and two room keys. I'll be expecting the rest of the rent by the end of next week. Oh, that's Thanksgiving. I'll give you until Monday. Send me a note when you have it."

"Thank you for that." I smile. "We really appreciate your flexibility."

When she's gone, James finally speaks. "This is pretty nice."

"Much better than where we've been staying, that's for sure."

"I hope you're right about this place. It's so far from everybody." He shrugs. "And so expensive."

"It was the cheapest, and the only one who got back to me. Let's try it out for a while." I empty my pack into neat stacks in two of the cubbies, then slip a strap over one shoulder. James' pile contains one worn, faded t-shirt and a pair of underwear. When I glance at his feet, bare ankles poke out above his sneakers. No wonder they stink. From my pocket, I pull out some cash and coins, and hand James enough for bus fare to get back and a schedule. "Your transfer will get you to work. You should arrive before your shift starts."

"It's gonna be pricey"—he looks at the money in his hand—"just to get to work."

"Maybe you can find a job around here." I try to sound encouraging.

"That's so hard." He frowns. "Robert found me this one. They pay cash, so I don't need documentation. And I don't have to pay taxes on it."

"We'll search together. I'll let you use my laptop. It'll be safer to be off the Hill." Not only for him. For me. I don't want him to lead anyone here.

"All right," he mutters. His focus lands on me. "Thanks for looking out for me, Rix."

I walk him to the bus stop and make sure he gets on, then dash to the other side to catch the 44 in the opposite direction. At this time of night, the Ballard Fred Meyer's my only option for cheap bed linens and towels, and maybe some socks for James. I also need laundry soap, bar soap, shampoo, toothpaste, and I could use some new socks as well. I'm under two hundred dollars. I doubt I can afford everything, plus save enough for Maggie's coffee on Tuesday. And, my transfer will get me there, but I'll need to walk the two and a half miles back up the hill to avoid paying another fare, so I can only buy as much as I can easily carry. It's a good thing I don't need money for food.

By the time James returns, the laundry's done, the bed's made and I already closed two tickets. "I see you found your way. The sheets are clean, so please bathe before you go to bed." I close my computer and look up at him. A red smudge on his cheek and spatters on his collar indicate he likely fed on his way back. "And try to not be so sloppy when you feed. We're around a lot of humans here. You need to be more careful." He looks down, like a sullen teenager. I lighten my voice. "I put laundry soap and towels on our shelf. And got you some socks."

He peeks into his cubby. "Thanks."

"Next weekend, we should get you some new shoes. When do you get paid?"

"At the end of the month, but I won't get it til the following Monday." When he pulls off his sneakers, their sour odor permeates the room. "It's a good thing we don't need to breathe." He gives me a chagrined smile. "I had to catch a bus as soon as I got off work, so I checked out the U-District. There aren't any students."

"They've gone home for the holiday. Here's more bus fare." I set a pile of ones and a large handful of quarters on top of the shelves. "So, I'm confused. You didn't feed?"

"Just the opposite." He smiles. "You should check it out. The place is crawling with street kids."

"Don't do that." Way too loud. My mind flashes to San Francisco in the late sixties, where the group I was staying with offered housing to a young homeless teen, and then passed him around as a party 'snack.' When I tried to stop them, they beat me and threatened me with a wooden stake. The kid lost so much blood, there was no way he could survive. Someone fed him some of their blood—then threw him out into the sun. To get rid of the evidence. It's why I moved to LA. I moderate my voice. "Never feed on kids, especially street kids. We have plenty of other options. If I find you doing it again, you're out of here."

November 26, 2019
Rix

By the time I trek the two miles to Lighthouse, drizzle from leaden clouds, dull in the fading light, causes my hoodie to cling to my shirt. In the warm glow behind the window, I spot Maggie at the cash register. As I enter, she turns, carrying two steaming cups. She points with her chin across the crowded coffee shop to a table with only one chair. "Grab that one." I take an extra chair from the next table, then hold it out for her. After setting the cups down, she raises her gaze to meet mine. "You really are a gentleman." Her face is radiant in the amber light.

I help her scoot her chair in, and sit across from her. "Thanks for the coffee. I thought it was my treat this time."

"You can get it next time." Her eyes twinkle with irrepressible mischief.

Next time? I return her smile. "You better keep that promise."

"It's supposed to drop below forty tonight. Will you be warm enough in just that hoodie?"

"The cold doesn't seem to bother me." Pulling off the jacket, I hang it on my chair, more to show off my new shirt than to let the hoodie dry.

"You look good in that shirt. Is it new?"

"No." Technically, it's used. "But all my t-shirts are in the laundry."

"You developers are notorious for your casual dress." She sips her eggnog latte. "I feel very special that you dressed up just for me."

"You are very special." Did I say that aloud? Maybe not. I drop my gaze to my cup. My knee bounces. "We make exceptions." Meeting her black pool eyes, I'm lost again.

She smiles. "Tell me about your week."

"Um." I blink. "It was fairly typical. How about you? Did you work any more ER shifts?"

"No, I took a break. I'm working through the holiday weekend"—she looks down at her coffee, and gives it a swirl—"to let the people with families spend it with them. My closest friend at the hospital will be there, too. So I'll have company."

"Wow. That's a generous thing to do."

When she lifts her head, her eyes glisten with tears. "It's better than spending it alone." Her cheeks darken. "I'm sorry. You may be spending it alone, too."

I force a smile. "I'm also working."

The fire of her fingertips on my hand causes it to reflexively jerk away. Her brows rise. "Sorry." She quickly withdraws her hand. "I'm not usually so forward."

Now both knees dance. I try to still them with my hands, then reach for my cup and take a sip. "It was just unexpected. You didn't do anything wrong."

"Your hand's so cold." She dips her head to look up at me. Her eyes follow mine as I lift my head and try to smile. Concern fills her face. "Are you all right?"

"Hyperesthesia." When she nods her understanding, I add, "Plus, some anxiety"—I wince—"that I'm working on."

"I'll try to remember that." She grins. "I love how you know the proper terminology."

"It's always good to understand one's idiosyncrasies." I pick up my cup, but set it back down. "Maggie?" The softness of my voice causes her to lean closer. "When did you lose your family?"

"Right after I turned six"—her gaze wanders around the cafe—"my mother just packed up and left us." She hesitates, bringing her eyes back to mine.

"I was eight when my father died." What am I doing? I've never shared this with anyone.

"My Dad died four—no, it's been four and a half—years ago. Pancreatic cancer." She looks at her hands, tan fingers tightly intertwined around her cup. "All wrapped around the mesenteric artery and vein."

"So unresectable," I murmur.

"Probably better that way." Her focus returns to me, and her fingers ease. Taking a deep breath, she forces a smile. "He stuck it out for two and a half years—blew away his oncologist—just so he could see me graduate. He died a couple of months later."

"That must have been difficult." I lean so close, her breath warms my cheeks. "I'm sorry he had to go through that."

"Thank you." Her face softens and glows a faint, affectionate amber. "You're the first person to ever say that. Everyone tells me they're sorry *I* had to go through that. No one else has considered what *he* endured."

The barista comes by to pick up our empty cups. "We're closing in ten minutes. You folks have a good night."

A chill frosts the outside air, especially after the humid warmth inside. Shivering, Maggie zips her jacket to the top. To not stand out as too strange, I zip up my hoodie and hold my hands under my armpits. That's a safe place for them. "This was really nice. I enjoyed your company." I nod over my shoulder. "I'm going that way."

She studies me with her brow pursed. "I had fun, too."

"So, can I put you on my calendar for next Monday? I can be here by five."

"Definitely. That'll give us more time to talk."

"All right." I back away a few steps. "Try not to work too hard."

"You, too." She doesn't move at all. "Goodnight."

I take a few more backwards steps. "Goodnight, Maggie May." Tearing my eyes from hers, I walk away.

December 16, 2019

Rix

On our little Brown Portable Record Player, The Waltz Orchestra's 'Waltz Dream' plays, scratchy now from being played so often. My wife, my Anna, smiles at me as we dance around the living room floor. I'll miss this so much after I've deployed. The rattle of a key in the door awakens me. I sit up and squint in the soft dawn light. When the door opens, I make out James' silhouette, backlit from the light that always burns in the hallway. He creeps in and shuts it quietly behind him before turning. "Oh, you're awake."

"Mm-hm. What time is it? It's already light."

"Almost eight." He shimmies from his jacket and kicks off his shoes.

"You're kind of pushing it, aren't you?"

"None of your business." Stripping to his briefs, he comes over to the bed. "Are you getting up?"

"Not yet, but why don't you sleep next to the wall." As he crawls past, the odor of sex, both male and female, wafts from him. I lie down and pull up the covers. Our shoulders touch in the too-narrow bed. "What are you doing out all night?" When he rolls away, I study his back. "I'm worried about you."

"I said, it's none of your business."

After trying unsuccessfully for an hour to fall back to sleep, I get up to shower. As I'm dressing, I notice the clothing James tossed on top of the shelves. The leather of the black jacket and jeans is light and supple. High quality stuff. The blood red shirt's as soft as real silk. How did he afford these? Is he prostituting himself? That could be dangerous, for him *and* for me.

Since I can't do anything about that today, I may as well study. I open my laptop. Having constant power and a relatively fast internet connection has been a real treat, enabling me to study during my afternoons and weekends. I enjoy it. My current lessons broaden my understanding of cluster management, hopefully making me more efficient at my job. And more employable. I wish I had additional storage space. Without a reliable income, cloud storage isn't a viable option. And a lot of the information I keep is too private for the web, even if I could afford it. After I get a little ahead, it may be time for new devices.

A text notification appears. From Maggie? She hasn't texted since last week when she canceled our coffee date.

> Hey, Rix.

How're things?

> Busy. But I'm free this evening. You up for coffee?

I'm surprised. I thought she lost interest.

Sure. What time?

> How about 4?

Sunset's not until four-eighteen.

I can be there at 5.

> Perfect! Looking forward to seeing you. :-)

To rest my eyes, and my brain, I flip open the book I've been reading, Trevor Noah's 'Born a Crime,' that I picked up in the tiny sharing library in the laundry room. It gives me a break from always having my head in my computer. I read for a while, then collect my dirty clothing. After throwing in a load of laundry, I dive back into my tutorial. When everything's dry, I change into my new shirt and best pair of jeans. I find a fraying cuff on my hoodie. That's the challenge in purchasing used clothing. Folding them both in half, I sew in new hems. The sleeves are now a little short, and it's a shabby contrast to my nice shirt, but this'll allow me a couple more months' use before I need to get another one. If the zipper lasts that long. I also need a haircut. The hundred dollars James gave me, apparently all that remained from his wages, didn't cover the cost of the clothes and shoes I bought him. He owes people money, or so he says, so I won't push him to pay me back. How did he end up so far in debt? Well, I guess partly by purchasing such nice clothing. His impulsiveness worries me.

James rises at four and goes to shower without saying a word to me. As he dresses, I ask, "How can you afford such nice things? Are you selling yourself?"

"Don't worry about it," he mumbles, then turns to face me. "Do you know Luna?"

"No. Is she new?"

"Yeah. She didn't make it back yesterday."

"What do you mean?"

"I mean she left"—he shrugs and pulls on his jacket—"and decided not to come back. Or the sun got her."

"Robert needs to be more careful." If he continues to transition people, he needs to give them adequate training. "Don't get yourself picked up, too. You remember what happened to Crystal." Unless ... was Luna abducted by those men? "*Please* be careful."

"I am. Has the sun set?"

"Why don't you have a phone?"

"Just answer the question."

I check the time. "Yes."

He disappears through the door, leaving it ajar.

I head out, pulling my hood up to keep my hair out of the winter drizzle. By the time I approach Lighthouse, I'm pretty damp. While I walk, I hum the last song on my playlist before I left, 'Demons.' Over and over. It's stuck in my head. I do need to shelter Maggie from the truth about me. Oh, no. Did I sing aloud?

"Rix?" Looking around, I spot Maggie approaching from the other direction. Did she hear me? The glow of her cheeks matches the warmth of her smile. "Was that Imagine Dragons?"

I nod. "'Demons.'" After we enter, I tell her, "You go sit. I'll order. It's a single tall latte, right?"

"Non-fat, decaf." She smiles as she tugs off her rain shell and shakes it out. "Make it an eggnog, please. Peter knows how I like it."

"'Tis the season."

When I turn with the steaming cups, I locate Maggie at one of the tables against the wall. Wending my way across the crowded shop, I squeeze between occupied chairs, careful not to spill. The couple at the other end of the table glance up, say "hi," and return to their conversation. After setting down the cups, I slide into the chair around the corner from Maggie. Pulling off my hoodie, I hang it on the back to dry.

Maggie rubs my shoulder. "You're soaked through." The heat from her hand lingers on the wet shirt.

"I'll dry."

"Where's your shell?"

Poking at a drop of spilled coffee, I shrug slightly. "How was your day?" When she doesn't answer, I raise my focus to her. "Has anyone told you, you have the most amazing eyes?"

"You're good at changing the subject." Her finger rises

to tap her upper lip as she studies me. "All right. My day was fine. The last patient canceled. That's why I'm here so early. And no." She smiles. "No one's ever told me that."

"I'm surprised." I continue to gaze at her.

"I was wondering"—she leans closer—"are you doing anything Saturday night?"

"Nothing planned."

"I'm meeting a friend at Green Lake at eight. To celebrate the Solstice. Let the last year go and welcome in the new one."

"Who's your friend?"

"Rama, from the ER. He's all alone, too. When he emigrated, he had to leave his family behind." She raises her brows. "Will you join us?"

"Sure. Sounds nice."

"Do you read much? What are you reading?"

"I picked up a copy of Trevor Noah's book."

"Oh, I've been meaning to read that." Shifting in her seat puts her knee against mine. She doesn't bother to move it. "Everyone says it's so good. How do you like it?"

"I like his entertaining writing style. You can almost hear him speaking. The story is impactful and sometimes tragic." She's so near, I catch her scent over the strong aroma of coffee. I inhale deeply to take it in. "Are you reading anything? Would you like to borrow it when I finish?"

"I would. I ran out of books and haven't had a chance to look for a new one."

When the coffee's gone, I don my still-damp jacket and follow Maggie out onto the sidewalk. She rubs her arms. "Brr. It's getting cold. Are you really warm enough in that wet hoodie?"

"I'll be fine."

"All right." Her frown turns into a little smile. "See you Saturday at eight at the Aqua Theater." She touches my shoulder, then turns to cross the street.

I hold my hand over the spot where her palm had just rested—reveling in the warmth—and watch until she disappears over the rise. "What are you getting yourself into, Rix?"

December 21, 2019
Rix

Time passes slower and slower as the week progresses. After cashing my paycheck and setting aside money for rent, bus fare, broadband connectivity and other essentials, my tiny stash of cash still grows to nearly eight hundred dollars. Even patched with shoe repair glue and lined with cardboard, my worn out sneakers—so cheap I was lucky they lasted this long— leave my feet wet each time I go out in the rain. I need some sturdy hiking shoes. I spend an evening hitting the thrift stores in the U-District with no luck. I haven't had new clothing in a dog's age—it's just too expensive—but I don't have many options. For the boots, especially if I get a good pair, I won't need to replace them for two or three years. And they'd be infinitely more comfortable. So on Thursday, I head over to REI where they're having an end-of-year sale. Two-hundred sixty dollars later, I walk out with the boots, three pairs of thick winter socks, and a rain shell. And an inflatable sleeping mat, just in case.

By Saturday afternoon, the rainy day has me antsy. Will Maggie call off the date? Right before sunset, the sky brightens and the constant drip, drip, drip from the gutter that lands outside the window dwindles, then stops completely by the time it's fully dark. At six-thirty, I head over to the lake. That should give me time to hunt before I meet Maggie.

I arrive at the Aqua Theater right on schedule and spot her sitting in the stands, gazing out at the lights on the water. She waves when she sees me. As I sit, she looks me over and smiles. "Nice jacket."

"I didn't want you to keep worrying about me getting wet."

Pulling some small squares of paper from her bag, she hands one to me. "We need to make our boats. Just do what I do." She folds the paper in half diagonally. "Now open it and fold the other two corners together." As she continues her instructions, I follow. She watches me for a moment. "You're pretty good. Have you done origami before?"

"It's been a long time. I used to do it with—" My voice catches. I see my daughter's six-year-old fingers fumbling to make the same fold for the same little boat. "Hold on." I lean close to see her paper. "Would you show me that last one again?" After studying me until I meet her eyes, she redoes the previous fold. I fuss with my boat. "Where's your friend … um … Rama?"

"He took an extra shift tonight."

"That's too bad. From what you've told me, he sounds like an interesting person."

She glances up. "We'll get together another time."

"Oh. I almost forgot." I reach into my backpack for 'Born a Crime' and hand it to her.

"Thank you. We'll compare notes when I'm finished." She tucks the book away and returns to folding. "We make one for each person we're missing. I need one, and three for Rama." She peers at me. "How many do you need?"

"Just two."

Soon, six tiny boats fill the area between us on the concrete bench.

"We're done." She smiles and reaches into her bag, this time pulling out a handful of votive candles. "These are pure beeswax." She sets a candle in each boat. "The paper's organic, so I don't feel too bad releasing them." Standing, she slings her bag over her shoulder. "Help me carry them down to the lake." She leads me to a spot beyond the glaring lights of the stadium.

At the water's edge, we squat. Pulling a lighter from her pocket, she lights each candle. We carefully let them go, one by one. I find my eyes on her as much as on the boats.

"We remember those who've gone"—Maggie glances at me—"and are thankful for those who are with us now." A slight breeze carries the little boats offshore. The tiny flames conjure an image of my mother's face, lit by the candles on a Christmas tree. Her smile is warm and full of her love for me. It must have been in Philadelphia, before we moved to the country to avoid the Spanish flu. In the end, that saved only her and me. Maggie leans against my shoulder as we watch our memories flicker across the water.

December 24, 2019
Maggie

As I scrub between patients, I yawn. From behind me, I hear a chuckle, and turn. Rama grins. "Are you going to make it until three?"

"Maybe." I stifle another yawn. "I'm glad it's slow and people are spending time with their families and friends instead of in here with us."

He nudges me away from the sink. "It's good we're working this shift instead of the early morning one when everyone's driving home from their partying." After drying his hands, he heads out the door. "It's time to eat. A Thai restaurant sent over a holiday feast. Let's grab a bite before it gets cold."

Plenty is left when we arrive at the table covered in food boxes. Taking a paper plate and some plastic dinnerware, I follow Rama through the line. Don't let your growling stomach get the best of you, Maggie. "I can't believe I'm eating so late," I mutter, taking only half the amount of rice I normally would.

As Rama scoops a portion from one container onto his plate, he grins at me. "Careful. These prawns are extra spicy." Pushing the spoon down, he lets it fill with the red-flecked sauce and drizzles it over his prawns. "Speaking of spicy"—he snags a spring roll and waits at the end of the table—"how did Saturday night go?"

"OK." As we sit at a little table, I keep my eyes on my plate and dig into the pad thai. "Mmm. This is really good."

"Just OK? Did you get rained on? Were you able to release the little boats?"

Nodding, I meet his gaze. "It was really quite nice. I'm sorry you had to work."

"Did you go alone?" Raising his brows, he lands his eyes on me while munching his spring roll.

"Rix went with me. He made two boats for himself."

"Ah. So his name's Rix. It's nice you weren't alone."

"It was." I take another bite. "I'm happy I'm with you tonight. The holidays get lonely when you're all alone. When I was really little, we sometimes—" A vivid memory of a Christmas Eve flashes through my mind. A fragrant tree with twinkling lights, surrounded by gifts. My Dad and mother kneeling beside me as we each picked one gift to open. My gaze drifts to Rama, who stopped eating to peer at me. "We sometimes had a tree. I miss that."

"That sounds pleasant." He eats his last prawn and scoops up some rice to chase it down. "Are you seeing Rix again?"

Choking on my curry, I cough and take a sip of the sweet milky tea the restaurant provided. "We didn't talk about that."

As soon as we return to the nurses' station, Rama gets pulled away to assist someone with a headache. Within minutes, I'm assigned to a man with a gash high on his left zygomatic, very close to his eye. I smile as I walk in. "Hi. I'm Maggie. I'll be your nurse practitioner." After logging in, I look over his chart. "Let's just make sure we have everything correct here. What's your name?"

"Bob Johnson." His voice is loud and gruff.

"Birthdate?"

"Seven twenty eighty-eight." A slight waft of alcohol reaches me, but his speech isn't slurred. He's unlikely to be drunk, but probably had a couple of drinks this evening.

"All right. Hop up on the bed." After he's lying on the half-reclined bed, I peel away the bloody washcloth he's been holding over his cheek and swab around the laceration to get a better look at the damage. "How'd this happen?"

"Erm." His angry eyes dance everywhere but me. Eyes so very different from Rix's gentle brown ones. What am I thinking? As I daub at the cut, he grabs my wrist with an iron grip, and barks, "Ow!"

"Please release my hand." I keep my voice steady and calm, like I've been trained to do, but my heart races. When he lets go, I open a gauze pad and place it over the injury. "Hold this." Going to the computer, I send an 'I feel threatened' message, *Please send assistance. Stat.*

By the time I turn back to the man, Rama slips in past the curtain. Wearing a smile that doesn't touch his eyes, he goes right to the man. "Let's get your BP." He tugs up Bob's sleeve and wraps the cuff around his arm, then flicks it on. As it fills, he comes around the bed to stand beside me. "Shall I have a look?"

"I don't think he needs stitches, but go ahead."

He presses his fingers to the gauze above where Bob holds it. "You can let go now."

"Are you the doctor?" He focuses entirely on Rama.

"I'm Rama, a nurse." Under the gauze, the wound no longer bleeds. He leans in for a closer look before turning back to me. "It's already beginning to bruise. I'll go get some ice."

While I wipe Bob's cheek to remove the residual blood, he doesn't react. I flick on my penlight. "Look straight at where the ceiling and the wall meet." After testing his pupil reflex, I check the blood pressure reading. "Your BP is one eighty-seven over ninety-eight. That's pretty high. Where does it usually run?"

He rolls his eyes. "I don't know."

"We'll check it again in a while. Injuries can cause it to rise, but I recommend talking to your primary care provider about it."

Rama returns carrying an icepack wrapped in a towel. "This is going to hurt a little." After carefully laying it over the purpling bruise, he places Bob's hand on it. He backs away, but waits for me.

"Bob, I'll be back to check on you in a bit." I logout of his file. "Please just lie here and relax. The ice should slow the swelling, but you're likely to have a black eye for a while." I follow Rama into the hallway. As soon as we're out of hearing range, I sigh with relief, and my tension leaves me. "Thanks for backing me up."

"I'm glad you handled it the way you did. He seems very tense. Did you ask what caused the injury?"

"That's what triggered him."

"Most injuries like this that I've seen were because of

being struck with a fist. I'd guess whoever hit him was wearing a ring. And probably male."

"He has a quick temper, but that doesn't mean he's not in a relationship with an abuser."

"Maybe he hit on a married woman in a bar, or it could be an extramarital affair. The possibilities are endless."

I shake my head. "I doubt he'll talk about it."

"We can only do our best." He smiles. "And you're doing just fine."

"Thanks. I'm glad it was you who came." My thoughts wander again to Rix. I can't imagine him being violent. What's he doing tonight? Probably working, too. "It's a shame these things happen on Christmas Eve."

4

TRUST

December 27, 2019
James
Content Warning for violence
See Footnotes for recap

After emptying the sanitary napkin disposal bin from the last stall into the big black garbage bag, I tie it shut. This is the part of my job that I hate the most, so I save it for last. Even though I just fed, the odor makes my stomach queasy. The bathroom door thumps open. "I'm cleaning," I holler. "I'll be out of here in a few minutes." Turning, I face Robert. Why is he here? "Uh ... hi."

"Do you have my money?"

I drop the bag. "You know I don't get paid til next week." As he moves into the tiny stall, I try to back away, but there's no room around the toilet. He takes another step and slams his fist into my gut. I grunt from the impact, and curl over. "What're you doing? I'll lose my job." I try to force myself upright. Using his knuckle, he jabs my forehead. The back of my head cracks against the wall. I nearly fall, but end up straddling the toilet instead.

From the hallway, Fernando calls, "What's going on in here? You all right, James?" His dark-haired head appears in the doorway.

"Back off, Fernando," Robert barks. "This is none of your business."

Even though I shake my head, Fernando ignores me. "Can't this wait? He's not done with his shift."

"Oh, yes he is." Grabbing my shirt, Robert tugs me along with him and pushes past Fernando. "He's done with this job. I'll send you someone else."

Out in the alley, he drags me with him, occasionally punching me in the arm or ribs. I reluctantly follow, stumbling along half a step behind. "I'll have the money on Tuesday. I'm sorry I'm late."

"You're always sorry." He backhands me. "Shut the fuck up."

I lick at the trickle of blood that oozes from my lip. Fear grips my gut. Maybe I should try to run, but Robert's faster than me. Safer to just go along with him. If he wanted me dead, he would've already staked me.

When we get to the new house, where the group occupies several basement rooms, Robert guides me into his and shoves the door closed. Whump. I smack into the concrete wall. His fist slams into my chest. The next hits my stomach, then my cheek. I know better than to fight him. He's way stronger than me. He continues to pound me. I raise my arms to protect my head, but then he punches me over and over in my gut and ribs. As I slide to the floor in a ball, he kicks my back and butt.

Grabbing my belt, he rolls me to where he can unfasten my jeans, and jerks them off. He yanks me to my feet and throws me onto his bed. I hear a zipper, and he forces himself inside me.

"You're hurting me," I groan.

He wrenches my head up by my hair. "Don't like it?" He thrusts. "Quit fucking with me. If you work the Hill, you work for me. You owe me eighty-five percent of what you've earned. I've been watching you."

When he rises and zips his pants, I tug up my underwear. He hauls me to my feet. I can barely stand. Using my jeans as a rag, he roughly wipes the blood from my face, then throws them into the corner. He draws me very close to whisper in my ear, "Rix always has money. Get what you owe me from him. Bring me at least five hundred tonight."

December 27 to 28, 2019
Rix

A thump startles me awake. I scramble to the corner and blink into the darkness. I make out James—who hasn't been here for the past four days—sitting on the foot of the bed with his head in his hands. "James, you scared me to death. Where've you been?" When he doesn't respond, I crawl across the mattress. "Are you all right?"

"Help me," he whispers, without looking up.

"What happened?"

"I'm in trouble," he whimpers.

"Hold on." Going to the desk, I flip on the lamp. We both squint in the sudden brightness. "Oh, James." He wears only his shirt, underwear and sneakers. One eye is swollen nearly shut. "Where are your clothes? Did Robert do this to you?" Is he sending me a message for taking James with me and leaving the Hill?

He drops his gaze to the floor. "Doesn't matter."

That's what my brother, Gareth, said the first time Alan beat him up—after Father left for the war—as punishment for not immediately doing what he was told. Robert's violence is accelerating in the same way since I left. Did I really influence his behavior that much? Should I have stayed? I was too small to protect Gareth. Can I protect James? Should I return to the Hill and take over the group? It's a responsibility I don't want, and would necessitate killing Robert. I don't know if I'm strong enough for that, even if I had the desire.

I put my hand on James' shoulder. "How can I help if you won't tell me what's wrong?"

"I owe some people some money."

"How much?"

"A lot. I need five hundred, right now."

"That'll wipe me out. I'm not sure I have that much."

"I can pay you back on Thursday"—he looks into my eyes, but his glowing cheeks tell me he's lying—"when I get paid."

"Go get cleaned up." While he's gone, I reach for my wallet and pull out four hundred-dollar bills and five twenties. That should keep James safe for a while. I'm left with forty-eight dollars. The comfort of feeling like I'm getting ahead evaporates. My paycheck should show up at the mailbox tomorrow, and I'll get one more on this contract even if Nalini can't get it renewed, so I'll be able to pay the February rent. That gives me a month's buffer to find a new position, if worse comes to worst. I leave the cash on the shelf above James' things and lie back down.

When James returns, he shoves his soiled clothing into a cubby, picks up the money and quickly counts it. "Thanks," he murmurs. Numerous red welts on his ribs will likely turn to bruises. After switching off the light, he crawls into bed. Turning away, he pulls the covers up to his ears, and begins to sob.

I roll against him and put my arm around his chest until he quiets, like I did with Gareth after Alan's beating. "Why don't you stay here with me for a while? Get away from the Hill?" He only shakes his head.

An hour later, he rises to dress.

I get up with him. "Where are you going?"

"I gotta pay tonight. Can I have bus fare?"

I hand him half a dozen dollar bills and a handful of quarters. "Be careful, James."

December 28, 2019
Rix

The dry, balmy weather continues. This has been the strangest winter, more like being in Southern California, but it makes hunting easier. People are out exercising instead of hibernating in their homes. As I head into Woodland Park on Saturday, Bryer and Cleve flank me.

"Hey, Rix." Bryer puts her hand on my shoulder as we keep walking. "Where've you been hiding?"

At her casual contact, my body stiffens, but I force a smile. "Working. And trying to stay out of trouble."

"Come join us tonight." She lets go. "We'll teach you how to hunt in a pack."

Cleve pokes me with his elbow, nearly knocking me off the trail. "Sorry." He grins. "I don't know my own strength. But come. You'll have fun."

"OK," I say halfheartedly. "What do we do?"

"Just follow along."

"It's similar to hunting alone"—Bryer moves ahead of us on the trail—"except someone's always watching your back."

After we enter the more wooded area, Bryer holds up a hand and points into a small clearing off the trail. Cleve takes my elbow, leading me behind the nearest tree. "We wait here," he whispers, then pulls me against him. I go rigid. "Relax. It's just pretend." He kisses my cheek. When a runner passes us, he drags me out to the path. Up ahead, Bryer leads the man onto a side trail. By the time we catch up, she already holds him in a vampire's embrace. "You're next." Cleve nudges me toward her.

Bryer pulls away from the man. She grins, gory and gruesome. Tiny droplets of blood hang from her extended fangs. I gape. Do I look like that? She lifts her hand from the wound. "Jutht take a little. Cleve'll be here in a thec." When a hand lands heavily on my shoulder, I reluctantly let go of the man. Cleve nods toward Bryer, who loiters near the main trail, where I join her. "Good job." She slaps my shoulder. "Now, we stand guard."

After returning to our original configuration, with Bryer well in the lead, Cleve asks, "Still hungry?" He smiles at my nod. "Don't worry. You'll get full. A smorgasbord of flavors."

As the night goes on, I begin to enjoy myself, as much as one can while biting people, and to appreciate how much more relaxed I am hunting in a group. These two seem genuinely fond of each other. I'm honored to be included in—what did Bryer call it?—their pack, at least for one night. Hunting takes far more time, but by the end, I'm pleasantly sated, like after a long holiday feast.

Near the exit, we sit on a picnic table, to let our meal digest and chat a little longer.

"So you decided to stay." Bryer scoots closer, until our thighs touch, and takes my hand. My stomach clenches. Her palm, the same temperature as mine, feels strangely cool. "I'm glad. Where are you staying?"

"Up by the freeway, a couple of blocks from Forty-fifth. I'm sharing a room"—I scrunch my face—"and a bed, with another vampire."

"So you're not involved with her?" She lets go of my hand to gesture with her palms up, then takes it again.

"Him. And no. I'm not involved with anyone." I frown. Is that true?

Cleve chuckles. "We'll see how long that lasts."

"Shh," Bryer shushes him. "Don't pay attention to Cleve. How's it working out, with you and your vampire friend?"

Is James a friend? I never really thought about him that way. "I'm working, but can't make ends meet." Why am I sharing this? Bryer's smile encourages me to continue. Is she enthralling me? No vampire has ever done that, that I'm aware of ... except the one who transitioned me, but those memories are vague. I don't want to think about that. I pull my hand away. "He promised to help with the rent, but struggles with impulse control and gets into trouble. I thought if I brought him with me—got him off the Hill, away from Robert—he might be able to turn things around, but ..." I grimace.

"What happened?"

"Not sure. He's in really deep. I gave him some money, but I'm worried he won't survive this."

"You're too generous, Rix." Bryer's hand goes to my knee. "But that's a nice quality." She shakes her head. "Vampires can be so unreliable."

"I can't argue with that." I frown. "You should know, there've been a couple of abductions up on Capitol Hill."

Her brows rise. "What do you mean?"

"I mean vampire abductions. One last November at the place where I was staying, and one about two weeks ago. In the first one, I barely missed being there. I saw men dressed in unmarked riot gear. I don't think they were the police. They had one of those big vans, like an armored car."

"That's not good," Cleve's murmur rumbles, close to my ear.

"Another reason to stay away from there." Bryer's voice is filled with disgust. "Maybe you should cut off your friend."

"Um ..." I blink. Should I? "I'll give that some thought."

A tiny smile tugs at her lips, accompanied by a flash of yellow confidence. She's beginning to trust me. "Thanks for letting us know."

I nod to the southeast. "The sky's getting light. I'd better be on my way." After lifting her hand from my knee, I give it a gentle squeeze. "Thanks so much for including me tonight." I look at Cleve. "I really appreciate you trusting me."

He touches my forearm, lightly this time, then hops to his feet. "We pick our friends carefully."

January 8, 2020
Rix

I shiver in the cold mud, unable to move, and try to keep my nose above the water. The shelling stops. Men squelch closer, speaking German. So, we lost the battle after all. Maybe, if I stay entirely still, they won't find me. If they do, I hope they just kill me. I do *not* want to be taken prisoner. Boots land inches from my head, splashing icy water over my face, making me choke and cough. "Hier ist eins." Bright light pulls me awake, spilling in from the hallway through the open door. Just as well to leave that dream behind.

James enters the room. "Sorry," he murmurs, and shuts the door. "Didn't mean to wake you."

"I just went to bed. Where've you been? I haven't seen you in a week." When he doesn't answer, I ask, "What time is it?"

"Four-thirty. Rix, I hate to do this again"—he sits on the bed—"but I need some more cash. Tonight. Right now."

I rub my face and sit up. "I can't keep doing this, James. I doubt my contract will be renewed."

"Please?" He puts his hand on my knee. "Please. They'll hurt me again."

"What kind of trouble are you in?" Turning, I drop my feet to the floor, breaking the contact with his hand. "Is there some other way I can help?"

He shakes his head. "I need another five hundred."

"Didn't you just get paid? What happened to that money?"

"I don't work there anymore," he mutters. "I've been prostituting myself." That's worrisome, given the current situation with abductions. I should ask him to move out. He's never here, anyway.

"So you're working. Why do you owe so much?"

"Don't ask questions I can't answer." He looks so distraught, I can't bring myself to throw him out.

"All right." I get up and reach for my wallet, glad I

stashed the rent money in one of my socks on my shelf. James watches me peel off five hundred dollars and return the remaining hundred-twenty to my wallet. When he meets my eyes, I hand him the cash. "I need the rest to pay for my phone and internet."

Shoving the bills into his pocket, he turns to the door. Before shutting it behind him, he glances over his shoulder. "I knew I could count on you." Maybe I *should* listen to Bryer.

After going to the bathroom to wash up, I login to my computer. May as well work a little since I'm awake. Picking up the second most important ticket, I dive in. When I next look at the time, it's nearly five, so I make notes and assign it to Prisha. She'll be going home soon. With only two days left on my contract, I've avoided taking on anything major, spending a lot of my time refactoring scripts and tying up loose ends. Nalini's in a meeting, trying to get an extension, but it seems unlikely.

Hey, John.

Well, speak of the devil.

Hi. How'd the meeting go?

No resolution yet. I should have word by this time tomorrow. Sorry it's taking so long.

NP. Thx for the update. Have a good night.

You have a good day. TTYL

I browse job ads, but find none that both match my skills and accommodate my schedule. Maybe things will pick up in another week or two, once folks settle back into work after the holidays. When Clarissa finishes her shower and heads out to classes, I start a load of wash— all my clothes except for the boxers I'm wearing. I set the timer for an hour, and lie down. Opening the book I just picked up in the laundry, 'On Earth We're Briefly Gorgeous,' by Ocean Vuong, I read the first few pages. Clarissa has an appetite for biography. This boy wasn't nearly as happy as the last one—exposing the demons that get passed from generation to generation. I guess vampires aren't the only monsters. I close the book, move my clothing to the dryer and lie down again, this time, to sleep. It takes a while. My mind won't stop jumping through the possible dangers of James' employment . If he's going to prostitute himself for Robert, I *will* need to cut him loose so he doesn't drag that mayhem to me.

January 8, 2020
Rix

At a little after three, the vibration of my phone on the desk awakens me. At first, I hope it's Nalini bringing good news, but then realize it's the middle of the night in India. I get up and thumb it open. The tension leaves my jaw when I see Maggie's name.

How are you doing?

I can almost hear her voice.

Good. What's up?

A limb broke on a tree in my yard during the wind last night. I need help cutting it, but won't be home until 5.

Couldn't be there before 5:30. Can we do it in the dark?

I have a floodlight in the back. Meet you at Lighthouse.

After I shower, I throw my sheets and towels into the wash, and fold my clothing. While I wait, I vacuum. By the time I make the bed, I can just make the rendezvous with Maggie. A bus passes me in the final block.

As I get to the corner, Maggie descends to the sidewalk. When she spots me, her entire face glows with her smile. "Good to see you."

"You, too." I follow her. "Where's your jacket? Aren't you cold?"

She rubs her arms. "I forgot it at work. At least, the wind and rain stopped."

"Now it's my turn to worry about you." I slip out of my hoodie and hold it out to her. "Here. You need it more than I do."

"Are you sure?" she asks as she tugs it on. I nod. She pulls up the hood and zips it to the top. "Oh, that's better already. I don't know what I was thinking when I left."

"The sun can fool you. How's work?"

"There's concern in China over an outbreak of a new

coronavirus. They haven't found the etiology. The WHO's getting involved, so it may be serious."

"How widespread is it?"

"In a week, it went from forty-four cases to a hundred twenty-one."

"So probably communicable." I frown. "Or worse, airborne."

"They should know more soon." She guides me around the next corner. "It's right down here. Did you do anything for New Year's Eve? It was too bad about the wind canceling the fireworks."

"I planned to go to Gas Works"—I shrug—"but weather."

"I was working in the ER. It was quieter than we expected, probably because everyone just stayed home."

"Do you work all the holidays?"

"Pretty much."

At the garage, I conspicuously avert my eyes as Maggie keys in the code. The door begins its slow rumbling ascent. Inside, she tugs off her shoes and my jacket—handing it to me—then dons an old pair of hiking boots, a well-worn flannel shirt and a faded M's baseball cap. From the seemingly random olio, she retrieves a power cord, reciprocal saw, pruning shears, and gloves and earplugs, handing a pair of each to me. "Let's go before it gets any colder."

A thin strip of wood anchors the limb to a large, well-established Japanese maple. Maggie squints up at the break. "Do you think we need the ladder?"

"Let's see how it goes."

"I'm going to lose some shade." She plucks at the branches. "I hope this didn't damage my fountain."

"Fountain?"

"It's buried under there"—she points vaguely toward the fence—"somewhere."

"That's only twigs. Nothing major. It's probably fine." After sawing through the branch nearest the break, I pass it to Maggie. "Can you cut that up enough to fit in the yard waste?"

She takes it and begins clipping the ends into the bin. "I'll do as much as I can, and we'll see what's left. Keep them coming."

Soon, the limb is barren of smaller branches. Its hold on the tree is strong enough to keep it from tearing or wiggling too much as I cut it into four foot lengths. With a final clean cut, I remove the last of it, sliding it down the side of the nearly full bin. Using the flashlight on my phone, I examine the wound, and run my finger around the edge to ensure it's smooth. "It should recover now."

A small stack of too-long branches sits off to the side. Maggie hands me a shears. "I don't have enough hand strength to cut through the thicker ones with this large clipper, but it should be able to handle them. Would you give it a try?" The sharp blade easily cuts through the green wood. And we're done. "You make it look so easy." As I start to gather the tools, she goes into the corner, mostly hidden by the surrounding shrubs. "Rix," she calls, "come over here."

I enter a tiny moss-covered glade. The noise of the city deadens, replaced by the trickling of water down a small stone fountain. Kneeling beside Maggie on the soft ground, I whisper, "This is magical."

"It's my safe place."

"Thanks for sharing it with me."

She pokes her finger into the flowing water. "I hate to turn this off, but I should drain it before the weather gets any colder."

As we walk back toward the house, I coil the power cord. "This was fun. I don't usually get the chance to work in gardens."

"I really appreciate it. I couldn't have managed on my own." In the garage, Maggie puts everything right back in its place. She does have it organized. "Can you stay for dinner?"

My mouth opens, and I start to say, 'I'd love to.' I *would* love to. What am I thinking? I don't even eat, although I am hungry. "I already have plans. I actually need to get going."

"Another time, then." She walks me to the sidewalk. "Thanks again. Have a great night."

January 9 to 10, 2020
Rix

Unable to sleep, I spend the afternoon giving my room a thorough cleaning. After showering and putting on clean clothes, I feel a little more settled. I drop onto the bed, and close my eyes. An image of Maggie kneeling beside her little fountain last night creeps into my mind, bringing an unexpected calm, as if I'm back in that magical place. I try to remember a similar feeling with my wife, but she was never so gentle, so open and caring. Not that I didn't love her. I still do. But times were different then. I was different then, young and full of optimism that I could make anything work out. If I had returned from the war, could we have worked things out? Life's never that simple. Especially now. I don't understand these feelings toward Maggie, but I feel so good when I'm with her. The vibration of my phone breaks my reverie. A tingle runs through my belly when I see it's from Maggie.

Hi, Rix.

Hi. How's it going?

Good. Wanted to thank you again for your help last night.

Any time.

Are you busy tonight?

Working.

Bummer. Rama's coming over for dinner and games. Was hoping you could join us.

Not tonight. Thanks for thinking of me. :-)

Well, maybe another time. I need to get dinner started. TTYL

Have fun.

How long can I manage to put off her dinner invitations? I set my alarm for eight, turn off the light and try to sleep.

I spend my first two hours of what I expect to be my final day of work reviewing recent tickets I worked on, and send my notes to Prisha, then update a few more scripts. As I check in the last one, my phone buzzes.

"Hello, Nalini."

"Hi, John. I wanted to let you know as soon as I knew for certain. I'm really sorry. We can't renew your contract. They haven't sorted out the annual budget yet. When they do, if you want, I'll try to arrange for a new contract."

"Please do." At least, the wait is over. "I'd love to work with you again. Any idea on how long it may take?"

"There's a lot of arguing going on, so probably not for a couple of weeks—" Her voice catches. "And that's more than I should've shared with you."

Have I charmed her with just my voice? That's never happened before. "Your secret's safe with me. Are you willing to provide a reference?"

"Of course. You've got my email. Don't hesitate to write."

"I appreciate that."

"I need to go. Don't forget to enter your hours before you log out."

"Thanks for everything. Goodbye."

"Goodbye, John."

Well, that's that. I have enough to pay for February

with a small reserve left for expenses, and March is covered by my pre-paid final month's rent, so I have some time. That's a luxury I haven't had in a while. Still, tension grabs my chest. I close the computer. When I tug off my hoodie, a faint whiff of Maggie wafts from it. I finish undressing, then reach for the jacket. Lying down, I snug the soft fabric against my cheek, breathe in deeply and begin to relax.

January 12, 2020
Rix

I'm really hungry tonight. Even though it's chilly, the dry weather should draw out runners and joggers, if not walkers. As I head down the trail toward the lake, a whisper carries my name from the shadows of the trees. Cleve steps from behind a large trunk. "Over here."

As I approach, Bryer's head pokes out. I catch the odor of cannabis. Behind the tree stand two vampires I don't know. "Oh." I study them. "I thought you were feeding."

Bryer indicates the two young men. "This is Matt and David."

The smoke from the joint grasped between Matt's pale, dusty rose lips wafts upward, disappearing into hair that hangs like straw over his thick brow. He stands nearly a head taller than David—probably not yet twenty—whose ashy brown cheeks carry a passionate glow as he smiles at me. After taking another quick drag, Matt offers the joint to me.

I shake my head. "Thanks, but it doesn't agree with me."

At footfalls on the trail, we all turn to watch a woman jog past. When she spots me, she waves, but thankfully keeps going. I wave back, then pivot to Bryer. "That's Maggie. She's off limits."

Peering after her, Cleve nods. Matt and David watch until she disappears around a bend, then turn to Bryer with questioning expressions.

Bryer smirks. "Possessive, aren't we?"

My focus locks on her. "Please." I try not to sound beseeching. "Leave her alone."

"Bry, don't tease." Cleve's voice resonates, even when he whispers. "Rix doesn't know you yet."

She punches his arm. "Quit sharing." Turning to me, she plucks at my pocket. "Do you have anything of hers?" She grins lasciviously. "Or maybe she's been all over you."

I bring the front of my hoodie to my nose and breathe in. Even though several days have passed, Maggie's scent lingers, easing the tension in my chest. I slip it off and hold it out. "She wore this."

Grabbing it, Bryer holds it up to her nose to inhale deeply. "Hm," she snorts, and hands it to Cleve.

He smiles faintly. "She smells nice."

When David sniffs the jacket, Matt moves cheek to cheek with him, using it as a curtain to distract him with a passionate kiss. David holds the jacket at arm's length, mouth still pressed to Matt's, and lets go. It lands at Cleve's feet. Smiling wryly, he retrieves the hoodie and hands it to me.

Bryer interrupts the kiss with an elbow to Matt's ribs.

"Are we all good, then?" After getting nods from the pair, she gives a tug on my sleeve. "Let's go hunting." As Matt and David head off along the trail to the south parking lot, Bryer leads me and Cleve down toward the lake. "We should find you a partner." She gives my upper arm an almost painful squeeze. "Don't worry about your woman."

January 15, 2020
Rix

A buzz in my pocket pulls me from deep slumber. Groggily, I tug out my phone and come more alert when I see the message is from Maggie.

> Got off early. Can you meet for coffee?

I rub my eyes and look up sunset. A quarter of five? Already? The long Seattle mid-winter nights are rapidly shrinking.

> Sure. But not til 5:30 or so. Does that work?

> Perfect. See you then.

Rain patters on my window. What's so important that Maggie's willing to brave the rain to get together? But it ends nearly as fast as it begins.

The walk in the cool, damp air helps clear my muzzy mind. When I'm sitting across from Maggie, with a warm cup between my hands, I stare dreamily at her while she tells me about her day, lulled by the familiar surroundings and the sound of her voice.

"Are you listening"—her fingers graze my sleeve—"or just watching me?"

"I'm listening." I give her a faint smile. "Just a little tired today. It's good China decided to share the genetic sequence. With the advancements in medical technology, maybe it won't take half a dozen years to get a vaccine."

"I hope it comes soon. On Monday, the WHO reported the first case outside China. In Thailand." She breathes in deeply, lets it out between fluttering lips, and takes a sip of her latte. "I wonder when our first case will be. We have so much air travel with China, it's probably already here and we just don't know it yet." When my fingers glide over the back of her hand, we blink at each other in surprise. As my hand creeps back to me, she smiles. I put my focus on my coffee. When I look up, she's still watching me. "Who were all those people in the park, a goth group or something? I didn't know you had so many friends."

"Just acquaintances, really." I shrink down around my cup, tapping the sides with my fingertips. A goth group? I guess most of us do wear dark colors. "Um ... Have you made any progress with 'Born a Crime?' Do you still like it?"

Her pursed lips ease into a little smile. "He's really quite remarkable. After such a rough beginning, he's come so far."

"His attitude has a lot to do with it."

"What are you reading now?"

"Another autobiography, 'On Earth We're Briefly

Gorgeous,' by Ocean Vuong. It's intriguing and well-written, but also a very sad story. I'm not sure I have the emotional stamina to finish."

"I've heard of that. I didn't realize it's so serious."

"He's the son of a Vietnam refugee who suffered through extreme trauma during the war. And her child was her only outlet for expressing her anger." I swirl my coffee. "Trauma leads to trauma."

"Maybe not the best read for these times." Maggie's fingers brush mine, then drift away like a wisp of smoke.

"Let's hope they don't get any worse." I attempt a smile. "This neighborhood has plenty of Little Free Libraries scattered through it. I'm sure I can find something lighter to occupy my mind."

"Or"—her radiant smile warms me—"you can have coffee with me."

January 18, 2020
Rix

The night's dry, and fairly warm, for mid-January. I change into an old t-shirt and pull on my hoodie, getting ready for the hunt. As I'm about to leave, James walks in, stumbling before he gets the door closed. "I need more money," he slurs.

"I can't."

"C'mon, Rix. I thought I could depend on you."

"I lost my contract. I only have enough for rent. Unless

I find something else, I'll need to give notice on this room before the end of February."

"Some friend you are," he hisses, then storms out, slamming the door behind him.

I reach to the back of my cubby and grope around until I find the pair of socks that hides the lion's share of my cash, which I shove into my pocket. I don't like to carry this much when I go out, but can't trust James to not help himself. And I do need to feed.

When I return, the room's a disaster, with the mattress turned on its side, and my socks, t-shirts and boxers strewn across the floor. I plunk down the mattress and make the bed, then pick up my clothing and set the chair upright. My nice shirt and my rain shell are missing. I scan the room. Where's my backpack? Oh, no! He took my laptop. How am I supposed to find another job without it? That's it. I'm done with James.

Plopping onto the bed, I stare at the ceiling. This definitely changes things. Buying new equipment will nearly wipe me out. I open my phone to search for refurbished computers, but don't find anything adequate for work that's available in the next couple of days. I look up the hours for the Apple Store at U-Village. Open til seven on Sundays. The sun doesn't set until nearly five. It'll be tight, but I should have time to get it tomorrow. If I don't find a job by Wednesday, when the rent comes due, I need to give my notice. At least, I'll have a month before I'm required to vacate, but I don't know how safe I'll be staying here. Or even in Seattle. It's time to move on to a new town. Portland's pretty close—and as an added bonus, their midsummer nights are longer than this far north. The thought doesn't make me feel any better.

I get up and grab the chair. Wedging it under the doorknob makes me feel a little less vulnerable, but I push the desk under the window to make it easier to escape, if the need arises. I change into clean clothing, tugging on an extra t-shirt and pair of boxers, then pull on my hoodie and slip on my boots. Just in case.

After turning off the light, I lie on top of the blanket, but only doze off and on through what remains of the night. Several times, I awaken, filled with hopelessness. What's wrong with me? I've certainly been through similar situations in the past. It's not easy, being a vampire. I know what's wrong, and shouldn't have let it happen. I was beginning to feel secure; to build trust with a new vampire community, and to trust them; and to enjoy the company of the woman with the amazing eyes. I'll miss Maggie most of all.

End of Volume One: Vampire Existence

VOLUME TWO: VAMPIRE HEART

1

FRIENDS

January 20, 2020
Rix

As my laundry dries, I set up my new laptop. After purchasing it, I have enough money left to rent a car, but that won't leave much of a buffer once I get to Portland. I look up train schedules and prices. Amtrak would be a little cheaper, but I doubt I can get to the King Street Station before the evening train leaves, and besides, if anything goes wrong en route, I could get stranded in the daylight. Maybe I should just talk to Bryer to see if she has room for me. Neither option quells the churning in my stomach.

My phone buzzes. Maggie has impeccable timing.

> Hi, Rix. What are you up to?

> Hanging out. How are you doing?

I'm good. It's been way too long. You free this afternoon or evening? Coffee? Dinner? Drinks?

Too long? It's been five days. I chuckle to myself. She eases my anxiety, even when I can't gaze into her eyes. I'm glad for this opportunity to see her one more time. And maybe tell her I'm leaving. I quickly check sunset.

Meet you at Lighthouse at 5:30?

I should be able to make that—if I hurry.

Perfect. :-)

We arrive at the coffee shop at the same time. Maggie loops her arm around mine. "I'm glad you could make it."

"Me, too."

"Hey, Maggie," the barista calls to her, "how're you doing? Want the usual?"

"Yes, please."

He looks at me. "Tall Americano, right?"

Smiling, I nod. I guess I'm a regular now. I turn to Maggie. "Go find us a seat. My turn to buy." After I pay and make my way to the table, I set down the beverages, then slip my new second-hand backpack, which holds my computer —I'm not letting that out of my sight again—under my chair.

When I'm seated, Maggie barely takes a sip before blurting, "The WHO produced a report on that new pneumonia virus in China. Dad would've been right in his element with this."

"He was an epidemiologist?"

"Virologist. I thought I told you."

I shake my head. "Is that why you went into medicine?"

"He wanted me to follow in his footsteps, but I wanted to be a doctor—to work directly with people. I got accepted at the U-dub Medical School the same week as Dad got his diagnosis. I would have had no time to care for him." She smiles, but it's a sad smile. "So I studied to become a nurse practitioner instead. It was still a lot of work, but we managed. And I got to spend a lot more time with him."

"I'm sure he was very proud of you." My comment sets her cheeks glowing in a golden radiance surrounding a genuine smile. I hate to bring her down, but ask, "You were talking about the WHO report. How bad is the virus?"

"They still don't know, but they're thinking about locking down Wuhan. Nineteen million people live in that city."

"That sounds serious. I hope they catch it before it spreads."

She sips her latte. "Did you lose your shell?"

"Um"—why can't I lie to her?—"actually, it was stolen ... by my roommate. He took a lot of my things before he moved out on me. I had to get a new laptop."

Her dark eyes grow wide. "That's terrible. How long have you known him?"

"A couple of years. He's been having a rough time. I let him move in with me hoping he might turn things around, but he runs with a bad crowd"—I hope she doesn't ask how I know him—"and got in over his head. I've been giving him money, but I couldn't give him enough, so he took what he could, and ran." My eyes wander.

"Why aren't you more angry?"

I return my focus to Maggie. "That doesn't help anything. People sometimes make bad decisions. I don't think they do it on purpose."

"That's a very empathetic attitude. I don't think I'd react that way."

"It's just a setback, but it compounded what had already happened." I frown. How did that slip out?

Maggie's face fills with concern. "What else happened?" She leans closer.

"I ..." I shouldn't share this. Gazing into her eyes, only inches away, I find myself unable to not tell her. "I lost my contract."

"What'll you do?"

"Look for a new job." Should I tell her I may move on? "I can stay where I am for another month, but I had to give my notice. I spent the rent money on my new laptop."

"I have a room you can rent in my basement." Maggie's eyes gleam. "It's all set up for it, with a separate entrance and a locked door between it and the upstairs. I just haven't had time to furnish it and look for a renter." It comes out in one rapid, breathless stream.

I stifle a chuckle. "What if I don't find another job?"

"I'll float you until you do. You need to stay somewhere. Besides"—she looks up through her long lashes—"what are friends for?"

"I can't believe James did that to me," I mutter.

"We don't always know people as well as we think we do." When I swirl my coffee, she puts her hand over my wrist, on the cuff of my hoodie. She's learning. "It'll all work out. You'll see." I study my cup. When she slides her hand down over mine, I barely resist the urge to jerk it away. She squeezes it softly. "Tell me you'll say yes."

After sipping my coffee, I look up—and fall into the depths of her eyes. "How much are you planning to charge?"

A tiny smile crests her lips. Letting go of my hand, she shrugs. "What are you paying now?"

"Eight twenty-five."

"Let's make it an even eight hundred."

The tension I've been holding inside eases. I guess I'll trust my gut. "All right. I'll move into your basement." My shoulders relax. A wave of calm flows over me. It feels like the right decision. "I'll have enough for the first month's rent after I cash my final paycheck. Hopefully, it won't take too long to find another contract. If I get behind, as soon as I find a job, I'll pay you for any missed rent, OK?" She smiles mischievously. "OK?" I repeat, a little more firmly.

"If it makes you happier."

"No pressure, but how soon do you think I could move in?"

"It needs furniture and paint." She frowns. "Are you in

a big rush? I thought you could stay where you are for another month."

"I can"—I wince—"but I'd rather move sooner, if that's possible. I can paint while you're at work." That should be doable.

"I like this plan. I can deduct it from your rent." She blinks as she thinks. "You've never been inside my place, have you?" When I shake my head, she slurps down the foamy remains of her latte. "Let's go there, now. You can check it out before you commit."

January 21, 2020
Maggie

Between patients, I fill my morning ordering painting supplies for Rix's bedroom. My late afternoon calendar is open, so I can be home to take delivery. As I talk to the rep about types of mattresses and how quickly one can be delivered, a tickle runs through my stomach. I guess I really *am* excited about my new roommate moving in. I add *get a key made for Rix* to my list.

As I type notes after my final appointment, a text arrives from Althea.

> You up for a half shift tonight?

Oof. That's going to be tight.

May be a few minutes late, but should be doable.

Perfect. See you soon.

Dashing home, I arrive only minutes before the Lowe's delivery truck. The well-organized crew quickly creates a huge stack of things, filling the center of Rix's bedroom. As they walk out, a van from Sherwin-Williams Paint arrives. I hope the colors match the rug I ordered. When the delivery person leaves, I scan the items, trying to ensure I didn't forget anything important. I check the time. If traffic's not horrible, I may still get to the hospital at the start of my shift.

My map app shows Interstate 5 as bright red southbound all the way from Northgate through downtown to Boeing Field. I risk taking surface streets through South Lake Union. With parts of Boren narrowed to a single lane due to high-rise construction projects, and blocks-long backups from the freeway onramp, it takes seventeen minutes to travel the six blocks from Denny to Pine where it finally opens up. At a red light, I text Althea.

Be there in fifteen.

My estimate is spot on, and I walk up to the nurses' station at six-oh-nine. From behind the counter, Rama looks up and smiles. "I didn't know you were coming in tonight."

"It was last minute. Am I not on the roster?"

He scans the sheet. "Oh, here you are."

"Quiet tonight?"

"So far. Let's hope everyone stays patient driving in the rain."

"It was only spitting, but traffic's awful."

"As usual." He grins. "You should move to the Hill. Then you could walk."

"Too expensive. I don't know how you afford it."

He taps a finger on his cheek. "It is. I share my one-bedroom apartment with a roommate, but our rent's more than most people in my home country earn in a year." He exhales an exasperated puff. "I don't know if we can still afford it if they raise it again. Too bad Seattle doesn't have rent control. That's the only reason my aunt still lives in New York City."

"This city's grown crazy expensive."

His eyes go to the computer monitor. "Here comes a child with a head wound." He smiles. "You're up."

From outside the examination room, I hear crying. As I pull the curtain shut, I say, "I'm your nurse practitioner. Similar to a doctor." While the woman tries to stifle her sobs, the girl—around five—stares at me with red-rimmed eyes, beyond tears. I login to her file. "My name's Maggie. What's yours?" I notice a man peering with concern from behind the woman. He puts his hand on her shoulder. Distraught parents. So far, so good.

"Sarah."

Her voice is so soft, I lean closer. "What's your last name?"

"Rodriguez."

"How old are you, Sarah?"

"Six. My birthday was yesterday."

"It was on Sunday." The man's calm voice carries a slight Latino accent.

"Are you her father?"

"Yes. Miguel Rodriguez, and this is my wife Helen."

I turn back to the girl. "Can you tell me what happened?"

"I hit my head."

"How'd you do that?" I examine the wound—a large purple lump, looking like an Easter egg. I'm glad it's not bleeding.

Her eyes leave me to wander around the room. When she brings them back, she whispers, "I climbed the cherry tree. I wasn't supposed to. Don't tell Mommy."

I send a request for an icepack. "And then you fell?"

"Mmm-hmm. Just like Daddy told me I would. Six isn't old enough. I need to wait til I'm bigger." Her eyes grow large when Rama enters with the cold pack.

"This is Rama. He's a nurse. Look at me." Clicking on my flashlight, I check for pupil reflex.

Sarah tries, but can't keep her gaze off Rama. "Boys can be nurses?"

"That's right." He gently lays the pack over her hematoma, holding it in place with his hand. "And girls can be doctors." She returns his smile.

"Did you bump anywhere else, Sarah?" I lift one arm, looking for other bruises, including older ones. Her hand and elbow are scraped, but not bleeding. I check her legs and find one knee has a bright violet bruise—nothing near the size of the one on her forehead. All consistent with a fall. "I'm going to look at your ribs and your tummy." After a more thorough examination, I'm relieved to find no other contusions. "Looks like you were lucky."

When we're together again at the nurses' station, several hours later, Rama smiles. Again. He always has a smile. "You're really good with children. Have you thought about having one?"

"Not really. I wouldn't want to do it alone."

"Maybe you'll meet someone." His brows rise. "Maybe someone like Rix. Are you still seeing him?"

My face grows hot. "We had coffee again last night."

"How'd that go?"

"He's moving into my basement bedroom," I blurt.

His jaw drops in true surprise. "That was quick."

"He lost his job and can't afford to stay where he is." I try to smile. "I've been thinking about renting out the room, but it was too much work to get it ready." I shrug. "He's doing all that."

"Take care with him, Maggie. You just met this man." After a quick glance at a new entry in the register, he pats my hand. "I'm up. I'll call if I need you."

January 22, 2020
Rix

I arrive at Maggie's a little before seven, bleary after two sleepless days and nights. My backpack bulges with my laptop, my inflatable camping pad that pokes out from the top, and whatever clothing I could fit between them.

Maggie peeks around my shoulder. "Are you moving in already?"

I keep my eyes downcast. "I just brought a few things." I'll bring the rest in smaller batches.

After standing aside, she swings the door open wider. "Come on in. Let's keep the heat inside."

A pile of painting supplies fills the middle of the basement bedroom: paint cans; brushes and rollers; buckets; plastic tarps; stir sticks; masking tape; plaster repair and spatulas; two ladders, complete with a long two-by-twelve to provide a raised platform; and paper coveralls and other protective gear. More may be hidden under these. I'm uncertain where to even begin.

"Text if anything's missing"—Maggie grins, voice echoing in the otherwise empty room—"and I'll pick it up on my way home. I hope you like the wall color. The lighter one's for the ceiling, and the off-white, for the door and the trim."

I smile at her enthusiasm. "This'll definitely get me started."

"Gotta go. Rush hour already began." And just like that, she disappears into the hallway.

I wish I'd asked what time she planned to leave, so we could have shared a cup of coffee, or just talked. The front door closes before my pack hits the floor. Tugging out the sleeping mat, I inflate it—no small feat for me—and place it against the south wall, in that triangle of shade where the sun never shines. I lie down and close my eyes, the safest I've felt in many months.

Droning awakens me with a jerk. I squint to take in my surroundings, then recognize Maggie's basement. A leaf blower outside is making the noise. I grab my phone. Already two-thirty. Maggie will be back soon. After moving my things into the closet, I begin covering the floor with plastic sheeting.

Well after dark, footsteps clomp on the front porch. Maggie comes straight down. "Looks like you got a good start." Her eyes dance around the room before dropping to the neatly sorted array of supplies.

"Not as far as I thought I'd be." I lay one last line of blue masking tape along a window. "I didn't want to begin painting in the afternoon, so just organized everything, did some masking and touched up the plaster. That's why it smells. At least, it already has a primer coat." I put the roll of tape in a bucket with the others. "That has a really strong odor."

"Properly prepping takes the longest." She grins. "That's what my Dad always used to tell me."

"I'll get an earlier start tomorrow so I can air the place out before you get home. It'll be in the fifties and no real rain's predicted."

"Sounds like a plan." Her smile broadens. "What're you doing for dinner?"

"Um ..." I can't have dinner with her. Human food makes me nauseous. And besides, I need to go hunting. "I'm meeting someone."

"Maybe some other time. Oh, almost forgot." She digs in her bag and pulls out a key. "This is for the side door. The garage door is keyed the same. Now you can come and go as you please."

"Thank you." I slip the key into my jeans pocket and grab my hoodie. "If you don't mind, I'd like to leave some of my things here." I gesture vaguely at my pack in the closet.

"Whatever works best for you. I can help you move the rest."

"I appreciate that, but I don't have much."

"OK. If you change your mind, let me know." Turning to the door, she gives me a little wave. "I'll stop down to say hi before I leave in the morning."

"See you then. Have a good night."

January 23 to 24, 2020
Rix

As soon as I'm up, I dash over to prep and get to work on the ceiling. I'm just sliding the two-by-twelve between the ladders when Maggie stops by. "Good morning." Her eyes grow large. "Those are really heavy. I was going to help with that."

"I got it."

"Don't hurt yourself. I have muscles, too. Just ask." Her face wears the faint blush of dawn. I can't hide a smile at her mixed emotions—a little fear, some anger, a lot of confidence. She glares. "What?"

"Just happy to see you."

"If you don't need me, I should be on my way." She returns my smile. "Have a good day. Text if you need anything."

The scaffolding makes applying the ceiling paint much easier than standing on a ladder. With the windows wide open—it's a balmy fifty-five; one of the benefits of global warming—I clean up, then lie down for a while late in the afternoon. I'm still not used to being awake all day and I'm deep asleep when the sound of the front door closing awakens me. I barely have time to stow my mat in the closet and start closing windows before Maggie appears in the doorway.

She smiles. "It's coming right along."

"I'll get the second coat on tomorrow, and Saturday I can start on the walls."

"I've wanted to do this for so long." A golden glow rises in her cheeks. "I can hardly wait to see it finished."

I can't remember the last time anyone's looked at me with so much affection. "I ... should head out," I stammer. "Have a good evening."

"See you in the morning."

The second coat goes on more quickly than the first, but takes longer to dry since it rains off and on all day, and I can only have the windows open a crack. I'm at the door, waiting, as the sun sets and dash out to catch the bus downtown. My final paycheck better be in my mailbox. If I hurry, I may be able to make it to the bank before it closes. Otherwise, I need to wait until Monday—and I'm nearly out of cash. Again.

The buses arrive when I need them to, and I'm on the Hill in record time. Mixed in with the junk mail are my phone bill and—yes!—the check. I slip them into the secret pocket I sewed inside my hoodie and zip it shut. As

I leave, I glance at the time on my phone. I still may make the bank. Abruptly turning outside the door, I nearly run into the person leaning against the front of the shop. I stop. "What do you want, James?"

He takes a step toward me, until our bodies nearly touch, towering over me. "You got paid."

Bracing myself, ready to spring away, I keep my eyes locked on his. "The check didn't come."

"It always comes on Friday."

"Well, not this time."

He moves nearer, trying to back me against the wall. He must be taking lessons in bullying from Robert—is he hidden nearby, observing? I hold my ground. James hisses, "You better not be lying." Shoving my shoulder, he strides away. He doesn't seem able to read my emotions. Hmm. Maybe, it's just me he can't read. Or maybe other vampires can't read emotions, either, or at least not as clearly as I do. It's not the kind of thing that's ever arisen in my rare casual conversations with vampires. I assumed we were all the same. But perhaps it's just my own oddness, which I always seem to generalize onto other folks before realizing very few interact with the world the same as I do.

I walk back to Fremont, changing my route several times to avoid leading James—or worse, Robert—to Maggie's. Losing the check would be one thing, but I don't want them to know where I'm staying. It's past midnight when I reach the house. I open the door as quietly as I can. After setting my alarm for five-thirty, to be up before Maggie finds me, I lie on the sleeping mat and close my eyes.

January 25, 2020
Rix

I'm hungry. More than hungry—I'm starving. I shiver. The prison uniform does little to protect me from the cold concrete wall that I'm shackled to. At a rustle, I spin to a crouch. And blink up at ... Maggie?

"Good morning." She waits as I drop my rear to the mat, then hands me a steaming cup of coffee, and sits beside me. "Did you sleep here last night?"

"Morning," I mumble. To give myself a few seconds to shake off the dream, I blow on the coffee before taking a sip. Didn't I set the alarm? "I was up, so I snuck in a while ago and then"—I shrug sheepishly—"I dozed off." Technically, that is what happened. I drink some more coffee. "Thanks, by the way, for the coffee." I attempt a weak smile. "It's just what I need."

She sets a muffin wrapped in a paper napkin on the mat between us. "In case you get hungry."

"Thank you." The crows will appreciate the treat. I look around the room. "I'll mask today. The walls will need two coats—at least. I hope to have it all cleaned up on Wednesday."

"Perfect." She nibbles her muffin. "The rug will arrive that afternoon. Can you be here when the delivery folks come? That way, I don't need to take time off from work."

For a moment, her gaze mesmerizes me. "Of course," I manage to croak.

"Oh, the chair comes on Monday. Can you be here for that, too?"

"Should be OK." I hope they're not too late. I still need to cash that check, but for now it's safely hidden in the closet.

"The bed and dresser, and pillows and linens arrive on Thursday. The movers will set it all up." She grins. "And then, you can move in for real." She's so pleased, and I try —really hard—to return her smile, but turn my head away, dropping my forehead into my palm. When she gently strokes my shoulder, I tense. "Sorry. I forgot," she murmurs, quickly removing her hand. "What is it? What's wrong?"

"Nothing." I raise my eyes to meet hers. "Everything's more right than you can imagine. I really appreciate all that you're doing for me."

"That's what friends are for." She peers at me, takes my empty cup, and smiles. I love her smile. "I'm heading to the store. Do you need anything?"

"I'm fine." I run my fingers over my eyes, wiping away the dewy tears that cling to the lashes. "I'll be fine."

Maggie comes and goes during the day, doing laundry, cleaning the basement bathroom and washing the hallway floor. Occasionally, she pokes her head in to check on me. "The bathroom's all clean. I put towels in there for you. The hallway closet has more. Feel free to use the detergent, if you need to do laundry."

"Thanks." A spatter of paint hits my cheek and drips onto the collar of my shirt. I smirk. "I'll need it."

As I put the last of the paint things away, Maggie appears in the doorway. "I like this color." She smiles. "What do you think?"

"It's very nice." I wouldn't have picked a golden peach, probably something on the grey side of blue, but then again, that may be because I haven't seen colors like this in so long. "Soft and warm"—my voice catches—"like the sky right before a sunset." Like the last sunset I shared with my wife before the war. I force the corners of my mouth into a smile. "I like it, too."

"Can you stay for dinner? Just some leftovers."

"Sorry. I have some things I need to take care of." I should feed tonight. I also need to pack my remaining clothing—if it's still there. And let Silvan know to change out the locks.

In the fading light of day, I feed the muffin Maggie gave me to the crows at the park. As I sit and watch while seven of them fight over the few crumbs, the mist condenses to droplets. The crows abandon the snack— except for one, who gobbles down the remains. Turning toward me, his head bobs as he calls, "Caw, caw, caw," before flapping up to join his group in the towering bigleaf maples.

I stroll down the main trail toward the lake. A hush fills the woods. Maybe I can find someone near the Aqua Theater. As I round the dog park, a rustle on a side trail grabs my attention. In the deeper shadows, I make out Bryer—standing guard, I guess. From behind a large tree, a little further along the trail beyond her, comes a muffled grunt. When she recognizes me, she gives me a small wave. Nodding to her, I keep moving down the trail.

By the time I get to the road, the drizzle turns to actual rain. I tug up my hood and head back to Maggie's. The house is dark as I slip quietly in through the side door. I still don't feel like I belong here. I hope that changes when I officially move in.

January 26 to 27, 2020
Rix

Around ten on Sunday night, I make my way from the woods to the picnic area on the south side of Woodland Park. As I approach, a person—no, a vampire—sitting on one of the tables hops to their feet. "Rix. Hold on."

"James?" Slowing, I scan the area for others.

"I been looking for you." He moves in front of me.

I stop, but my eyes continue to scour the woods around us. "What do you want?"

"I want that money."

"I don't have it." I square my shoulders. "And if I did, why would I give it to you? You already owe me several thousand dollars."

"I need it more than you do."

I take a step to the side, but he moves to block me. When he shoves me backwards, I nearly lose my footing on the uneven trail.

"Hi, Rix." Bryer's voice comes from behind me. "Everything alright?"

I glance over my shoulder. When Cleve approaches on my other side, James' mouth drops open. "Just ran into an old roommate." I hold his eyes. "Everything's fine."

Bryer puts her hand on my shoulder. "We won't be far."

I take another quick peek at her. "Nice seeing you again. Good hunting." As the pair heads off into the woods, I hold out my hand to James. "Give me your keys. I need to return them to Silvan."

"We still have the room for another month."

"I still have the room. You gave up your right to be there." I flex my fingers in an impatient gesture. James stares after Bryer and Cleve, then digs in his pocket and drops the keys into my outstretched hand. "I'd suggest you stay away from this neighborhood. I'm sorry things didn't work out better for you. Try not to get yourself killed." I walk past him without looking back.

I'm not surprised to find the room ransacked again. Every cubby is empty, the mattress is overturned, and the desk drawers lay strewn on the floor with what little remains of my clothing. I spend the next hour putting everything back in order, and folding and packing my jeans, two t-shirts, a couple of pairs of socks and underwear, and the blanket. My backpack won't hold another sock. I'm not supposed to run laundry at night, so leave the sheets in a pile in the middle of the mattress—they're for a double anyway, and Maggie ordered a queen. If I never come back, Silvan can decide what to do with them.

Then, I sit on the bed, with my back against the wall,

and wait. Around two, my head starts to bob. I struggle to keep my eyes open. The vibration of my phone brings my head up so fast, it thumps into the wall behind me. "OK," I mutter, "I'm awake."

I thumb open my phone to find a text from Nalini.

Hey. Long time. How's it going?

I'm doing well. How are things in Mumbai?

They finally finished the annual budget and some was allocated for DevOps contractors. I'm pulling together a new team. It's half-time for a two month contract, like before. Are you available to start February seventeenth? It's the earliest they would allow.

That's doable.

Good. Looking forward to working with you again. We've missed you. I'll send paperwork soon. TTFN

Thanks for thinking of me. Talk to you soon.

January 27, 2020
Rix

By five-thirty, I can no longer sit still. Hopefully, James is long gone, but I keep a wary eye out as I walk, changing directions several times. Because of all the detours, what should have been a two-mile route takes me an hour and a half to walk. I meet Maggie as she's leaving.

"Good morning." She smiles. I love her smile. Her expression turns to concern. "Are you all right? You look tired."

"I didn't sleep well"—I shake my head—"but that's not too uncommon. I'm kind of a night owl."

"Maybe you'll have time to take a nap before the chair's delivered—between three and four. Will that still work for you?"

"Sure. That should be fine." I give her a half smile. "Guess what? I found a contract. I start on the seventeenth."

"See, I told you everything would work out." She beams, as if it was all part of her plan. Was it? "Aside from all the worry you went through, you ended up here."

"That *is* the best part."

"I gotta run or I'll be late. Text if anything comes up. Will I see you this evening?"

"I still have some loose ends to tie up, but"—I look over my shoulder at my backpack—"I kind of brought the rest of my things, so I was hoping to sleep here tonight. If that's OK with you."

"Of course, but the bed won't be here until Thursday. In the morning, they promised."

"I'll be fine." I nod. "I've got my sleeping mat and a blanket. I'll try not to wake you when I come in."

She crinkles her nose. "What about the odor?"

"I should be OK. If it bothers me, I'll crack open one of the windows." I hope my smile looks confident.

"All right." Her serious face softens. "But promise you'll text me if it's a problem."

"I promise."

As I clean the brushes and rollers, a text tells me the chair is here. I open the garage door, and the delivery guy brings it all the way to the back. He hands me a tablet and stylus to sign. "Let me know as soon as possible if anything's not right."

"Thank you. We will." I hand the device to him, and he's on his way.

When I go back to the room, I pull out my mat and blanket, and set up a bed near the south wall—so I don't need to worry about the sun—plugging in my laptop and phone next to it. As soon as I sit, fatigue hits me. I roll to my side, intending to set an alarm for four-thirty, but my eyes slam shut.

Light rapping pulls me from a deep sleep. "Rix?" Maggie calls softly, peeking in at me from the door.

"When did it get dark?" I mumble as I roll to sitting.

"About two hours ago. Can I come in?" When I nod, she enters and closes the door. "Brr. Aren't you cold?" Going to each window, she latches them shut.

"I meant to close those before it got this late." I fold my blanket.

"Sorry I woke you." She sits next to me on the mat, so close I can feel her body heat. "You said you were planning to go out."

"I am. I dozed off. Thanks for checking on me."

"Maybe you should just sleep."

"I won't be gone long." I reach for my phone. "I'll sleep when I get back."

"All right." She gets to her feet. "The room is great. Thanks for all your hard work." From the door, she looks back. "See you in the morning."

I get up and pull on my hoodie. From its hiding place in the closet, I retrieve the check and slip it into the secret pocket. As soon as I'm outside, the cool air brings me fully awake. I'm glad the rain stopped. It's only a mile to the Fred Meyer, where I discovered I can cash a payroll check until nine for a three dollar fee. It's worth the cost, since I'd need to pay nearly that much in bus fare to get to the payroll company's bank on Capitol Hill before it closes. I'm avoiding the Hill, anyway. The numerous routes I can take to get to the store—all residential—make me feel even safer.

When I return, a sleeping bag, pillow and small pile of hangers sit outside the door to my room, even though I left the door wide open. After I hang my hoodie in the closet, I strip, take a quick shower and snug into the downy softness. Warm and safe, I drift into peaceful sleep.

January 29, 2020
Rix

On Wednesday, I remove the last of the masking tape and pick up the plastic drop cloth. By two-thirty, I finish washing the floor. The open windows dry it well before the rug is delivered. As I stow the last of the supplies in the garage, I consider how to organize the increasing accumulation of stuff in here. With the copious boxes, gardening tools, cleaning supplies, and now, the paint cans, brushes and tarps, there's barely space for Maggie's car. I'll ask her to order some shelving.

The delivery truck driving up pulls me from my planning. I left the garage door open, and the driver finds me. He and his helper make quick work of laying the pad and rug, and within fifteen minutes of arriving, they're gone.

Maggie has a good eye for colors. And a taste for high-quality merchandise. The rug is amazingly thick and plush. Flecks of the peachy-gold from the walls, the paler shade from the ceiling and even the off-white trim—all stolen from the glow of a sunset—pop in its dark, intricate pattern. I remove my shoes by the door, then run the vacuum over it. As I turn it off, I spot Maggie standing in the doorway and pause to gaze at her. "Just finishing."

She kicks off her shoes. One lands on top of mine. I stifle my cringe. Walking onto the rug, she turns around to take in the room. "Perfect. The paint job looks professional."

"Thank you." One of the many skills I mastered doing odd jobs over the years.

Squatting, she runs her hand over the soft wool and grins up at me. "What do you think?"

"It's quite elegant." I catch myself before I add, 'You didn't need to spend so much,' deciding to let her enjoy the moment. She's obviously never rented out a room before. "The colors go really well together."

"I can't wait to see it with the furniture."

I finish coiling the vacuum cord. "Let me put this away, then we can talk, if you want."

She smiles impishly. "I'll be back in a sec."

As I head over to the bathroom, I neaten her shoes. I wash my face and arms, and run my fingers through my hair. It will have to do. The clink of glasses draws my attention. "I'll be right there," I call.

By the time I enter the room, Maggie's sitting cross-legged in the middle of the rug beside a small tray holding six votive candles in tiny glasses. "Turn off the light." She lights the last wick. "This is so cozy. Would you open the bottle? Do you drink wine?"

Sitting across from her, I reach for the bottle and opener. "Only on special occasions."

"This *is* a special occasion."

As I read the label, my brows rise. I'm beginning to comprehend the extent of her wealth. I cut off the foil and twist in the corkscrew. "Nice wine." When I glance up at her, I'm enthralled.

"What are you waiting for?" She grins, face radiant in the soft candlelight. "Open the bottle. Let's celebrate." Blinking, I put my attention back on my task. When we both hold half-full goblets of deep red liquid, she says, "To friendship."

I tap my glass against hers, and smile. It feels … natural. After sniffing, I sip the robust wine and swish it in my mouth, then swallow. "Very nice." I raise my glass to her. "To good friends."

2

DEATH

January 31 to February 7, 2020
Rix

Over the next several days, I adjust to my new living arrangement. I haven't lived in such luxury in ages. It's almost too quiet, but I don't mind. Even Maggie has let me be, although I occasionally hear her in the laundry room or puttering around in the garage. I read or watch tech videos, but have trouble focusing, so spend most of my time asleep.

Now that I found a safe haven, I'm reluctant to venture outside—afraid of being discovered. On Tuesday, I run down to set up a new box at Ballard Mailbox—even though it's just over a mile away, I barely have time to get there before they close. Since Ballard Avenue is on the way back, I check it out. Despite it being Tuesday, it's crowded. The trick is finding someone whose blood alcohol level isn't unpalatable. At least I don't need to taste test them—I can tell by just their smell. I lurk in an alley until a designated driver ducks in for a smoke. I dislike nicotine-tainted blood, but I'm too hungry to pass up this opportunity. After drawing him into a dark corner behind the commercial-sized recycle bin, I feed for only a short while before more smokers arrive.

"Craig, where are you hiding?" one of them calls as they light up.

Even though I'm not sated, I let him go. It'll do for tonight.

By Friday afternoon, my stomach tells me I need to go hunting again, but it's raining—really hard. The sun sets. I make no move to go out. No point in going to the park, and I don't relish the thought of feeding on the Ballard crowd again. Maggie comes home. After she runs the vacuum, the house returns to quiet. I doze again. Her footsteps in the stairwell awaken me, and the washer begins to fill. She knocks on the door at the end of the hallway. When the key rattles in the lock, I get up and straighten the sheets, then tug on a pair of jeans. Maggie knocks on my door. "Rix? Are you OK?"

"Hold on." As I pull a wrinkled t-shirt over my head, I open it.

"Hi." She gives me a faint smile. "I hate to intrude, but I haven't heard a peep from you in a few days. I just wanted to make sure you're all right."

Opening the door a little wider, I wave my hand to welcome her. "Come in." I indicate she can have the chair, and sit on the rumpled bed, drawing my knees up to my chest. "I didn't mean to cause you con— ... to make you worry. How are you?"

"I'm good." She sits. "You're so quiet, I wasn't sure you were even here."

"I've slept a lot." I attempt a reassuring smile. "I was more exhausted than I realized."

She leans forward to scan my face. "You look less tired." When her hand begins to rise toward me, she quickly withdraws it. An expression I can't decipher—embarrassment? confusion?—flits across her face, and she retreats back into the chair. "Are you comfortable down here? Do you have everything you need? Is the little fridge working OK? I noticed it's empty." She's back on the edge of her seat, and I find myself tensing with her. "Have you been eating all your meals out? I'm reheating some pizza. Would you like me to bring some down for you?" When she realizes she hasn't given me a chance to answer one question before hitting me with the next, her eyes grow large and her cheeks radiate a ruby blush. As I gaze at her, bemused, I begin to relax. No one else has this effect on me. "I'm sorry. I don't know what gets in to me"—she looks down—"when I'm around you."

"Maggie." When she meets my eyes, my smile surprises me. It's the first genuine one I've given anyone in a very long while—even her. "I'm fine. Everything's perfect." Her smile enthralls me. I'm not certain what I'm feeling. She seems equally enchanted, but I have that effect on people. I force my eyes away. "What've you been up to?"

"Mostly working. I'm still reading Trevor Noah. His

stories are so funny—like the one about pooping in the kitchen." She laughs.

"Ha ha. That was a good one. He must've been a handful."

"Have you been keeping up on the news from China?"

"You mean the virus?"

"Yes. They've had over two hundred deaths, and it's spreading internationally."

"I wonder how long before it reaches here." This time, it's me who moves closer. I drop my feet to the floor and lean on my elbows. "Are the hospitals here prepared?"

"Seattle's pretty well situated, but we already had a confirmed case last week—up in Everett. The first in the nation."

"It'll be interesting to follow."

She crinkles her nose and chuckles. "You sound just like my Dad."

"I hope you're not at too great a risk, working face to face with patients, particularly in the ER."

"We're taking more precautions." She frowns. "But, we started rationing N95 masks, in case the supply chain dries up."

"The Government should have emergency stockpiles, right?"

"Let's hope so." She gets to her feet. "I'm glad you're settling in. I feel more comfortable—safer—knowing you're living down here."

I stand. "I ..." I don't want her to leave yet. "I'm really happy to be here."

At the door, she turns. "Text me if you want some

coffee in the morning." She shuts the door, and I'm alone again.

February 8, 2020
Rix

At a little after seven, Maggie texts.

> Good morning. Since it's Saturday, I'm thinking of going to Lighthouse to see if any room is left to sit. Wanna go?

> Gathering laundry, if you aren't doing any this morning. I'll have to pass.

I continue sorting it into two piles. I usually don't have enough to require more than a single load, but now big, fluffy towels and queen-sized sheets augment my meager collection of clothing.

> We'll do it a different time. How about a cup of coffee here with me? I miss our talks.

> Me, too.

Avoiding her is becoming more difficult. And I don't really want to.

> That sounds nice. Will you join me in my room?

Be right down. :-)

By the time I start my first load and return to my room, Maggie arrives carrying a tray with a thermal pitcher, two mugs and a plate of pastries. She sets it on the bare mattress, then sits next to it, drawing her legs into the lotus position. Smiling up at me, she pats the bed. I sit facing her, with my back resting against the headboard and my arm wrapped around a knee.

She begins to pour, then glances up. When she looks down again, her brows shoot up, and she abruptly pulls the carafe upright. The cup she offers—filled to the brim—draws my eyes from her face. "Careful," she murmurs, "I filled it a little too full."

I reach for it with both hands and sip it to a safer level, then raise my eyes to meet hers. "Aren't you going to have any?"

After tearing her gaze from me, she reaches for an almond croissant, cradling it in a napkin to catch the copious crumbs. "Mm. I love these." Powdered sugar dusts her lips, like hoarfrost on a brisk New England dawn. "Do you want one?"

"I'll just drink coffee."

She studies me, then takes a sip from her mug. "You're so thin. Do you ever eat?" When I frown and look down at my cup, she sets her pastry on the tray and quickly licks her fingers before wiping them with a napkin. "I didn't mean to pry." She leans toward me.

I watch her fingers touch my knee, so don't recoil. "A lot of food doesn't agree with me." Glancing up at her, I take another sip of coffee. "The coffee's good. Thanks for bringing it." When she slides her hand onto my thigh, just above the knee, I put mine over hers. This time, it's her who doesn't recoil—holding the coffee cup warmed my hands. "Don't worry so much about me. I'm a mixed bag of medical conditions."

She seems content with the small amount of physical contact and my tiny confession. "What're your plans for the day?"

"Laundry and cleaning." I reluctantly remove my hand. "Then, I'll sleep some more. What about you?"

Sitting back, she resumes eating her croissant. "I'm taking an ER shift. Rama will be there, too. After work, we're planning to eat up on the Hill, then he's coming by for a while—to play games or watch a movie or just hang out." She sips her coffee and puts her focus on me. "He's been asking to meet you. Do you want to join us?"

"I ..." My eyes blink as I mull it over. "I'm not sure yet." Socializing with strangers is likely a bad idea, especially since I haven't fed in several days. It's hard enough to sit here with Maggie, but I would never bite her.

"No pressure."

"Oh. I forgot something. Wait here." Setting my cup on the tray, I roll to the far side of the bed and go to the closet. "Look what I found in the garage." I hand her a box, a little larger than a tissue box. "N95s. A new box of a hundred."

"This should last me and Rama for two months"—her misty eyes shine and her cheeks glow with rosy warmth—"if we run out at work. Thank you."

"Thank your dad. I'm sure he left them for a situation just like this." It's is no surprise, coming from a virologist.

"What's this?" She worries the corner of a folded paper from under the lid and opens it. Her aura swirls with the greens of grief and golds of pure love.

"What is it?"

"A note." She takes a shaky breath.

My sweet Maggie May, For the next pandemic, since I won't be here to protect you. I'm sure it's right around the bend. Stay safe. All my love, Dad.

After daubing at her eyes, she picks up the remains of her croissant and pops it into her mouth. She finishes her coffee, then rises, giving me a little smile. "I need to get some things done before I leave." She picks up the tray. "Thanks again for finding the masks."

"Text me later"—I scramble to my feet—"about tonight?"

Her smile broadens. "We should do this again. Next time, join me in the kitchen."

February 8, 2020
Rix

My hunger drives me out into the wet night. I should feed more often—even Maggie notices how thin I am—but last night was stormy and tonight was forecast to be calmer. I try to keep it to a minimum, but after five days, I get weak and queasy—and it's already been four.

The inclement weather forces me to find somewhere to feed indoors. A restroom stall at a singles bar is an innocuous place to loiter without needing to purchase a drink. I'll never understand how people afford the exorbitant prices. A lone man walks in and goes to the urinal. My phone vibrates. In the time it takes to read the message from Maggie asking if I want to join her and Rama watching a movie, another man walks in, and I've lost the opportunity. The first man leaves—ugh, without washing his hands—but another enters before the door shuts.

Sorry. Not tonight. Thx anyway.

I click send. With two flushes, the room empties. Three men enter in quick succession, and there's never fewer than two pissers at a time. My feet begin to ache. Maybe I should find a less popular bar. The last group exits. I step onto the toilet rim to squat for a while. As I'm about to return to standing, two people walk in. I stay put.

A woman giggles, then slurs, "You sure?" She stumbles, then giggles some more. "Oh, is that where you pee-pee?"

"Let's go in here." The door to the handicapped stall bangs into the wall that separates us.

"I dunno about this."

"Don't worry." A zipper zips. "This happens all the time in here."

"OK." Her voice sounds young and innocent. "If you say so." Has she been slipped a roofie? I should intervene, but that may bring an altercation—and cops. I can't afford the risk. I'm stuck, squatting on the toilet, until his grunts and moans fade, and they leave. Stepping down, I shift from foot to foot until I can feel my toes again.

A man enters. I wait for him to finish at the urinal, then make my move. He doesn't notice me until I'm beside him at the sink. When his head turns toward me, I run a finger along his jaw. He gapes. "Why don't you join me over here"—I move into the handicapped stall—"where it's more private."

Like a lost puppy, he follows me, reminding me of the woman, just as willing and helpless. Another necessary evil, Rix. I push the thought away and latch the door. It's too busy for me to feed for long. I let him go before I'm sated, but at least my stomach no longer growls. After he leaves, I thoroughly wash my hands and face, then check for any flecks of blood on my clothing. I'm done for tonight. It's too stressful feeding like this. The forecast says it should be dry by Monday, so I can go to Woodland Park.

I trudge back to Maggie's in the drizzling rain. Even with my new shell, my hoodie and jeans are wet when I arrive a little after one. The house is dark. I slip inside, strip and throw the moist clothes into the dryer. At least my boots kept my feet dry. Since my hair's already damp, I take a quick shower—the hot water feels nice—and drop into bed. A nice bed, in a nice room, in a very nice house. I feel incongruous, like I don't belong. Like I don't deserve to be here. Like a vampire shouldn't be in such a place. I lie in the dark, staring at the ceiling, until the shuffle of Maggie's slippers upstairs and the faint dawn light announce the arrival of the new day.

February 17, 2020
Rix

Filling out paperwork and the new employee orientation Zoom meeting take up all of my four allotted hours my first day on the job. I don't log off until after five. Going hunting crosses my mind, but the nights are already getting shorter. Why risk being out at sunrise, which is around seven these days? I can hunt before work tonight. Too awake to sleep, I scan news headlines.

A text alert distracts me from my reading, making me smile. It's from Maggie.

Are you awake?

doomscrolling

Join me in the kitchen for coffee?

up in a few

This is new. Stopping in the bathroom, I brush my teeth and comb my hair. I probably still look rumpled, but at least my breath should be more minty. I have no idea how offensive my breath is, but with Maggie, I worry about it. At the top of the stairs, I knock.

"It's unlocked," she calls. "Come on in." When I step into the kitchen, she smiles—love her smile—sets two steaming cups on the island and sits.

I slide onto the stool next to her and take a sip from the nearest mug. "You make the best coffee."

"It's Lighthouse Ethiopian." Raising the cup, she blows on it before taking a drink. "Nice and dark. How'd your first day of work go?"

"Pretty much as expected. Lots of paperwork and boring meetings. I won't get any real work done for a couple of days."

"Congratulations anyway."

"Thanks. How's work going for you?"

She takes a deliberate swallow. "About the same, but there's a lot of worry about the new virus. The WHO named it COVID-19"

"I was reading about that." I nod. "Two thousand people have died from it already. But not here yet."

"Not yet." Her eyes drop to her coffee. "On Friday, they reported more than seventeen hundred healthcare workers in China have been infected, and at least six died."

"Hopefully, they'll get a handle on it before it spreads here." I touch her shoulder.

"They're planning for us to go remote, at least part-time." She shrugs. "So, work with my patients online. That'll be strange."

"See? Planning. Time's on our side." I give her an encouraging smile. "There's no reason for a major outbreak in America."

"This is a nasty disease." She crinkles her nose, causing me to stifle a smile at the gesture. "I wish the government would quit downplaying it. A lot of people likely won't take it seriously."

"You may be right. Let's hope it doesn't come to that." After draining my cup, I set it on the countertop. "Full day ahead?"

"Booked end-to-end." She scoots off her stool. "Do you want another cup?"

I put my hand over my mug. "I shouldn't or I may not get any sleep."

After filling her cup halfway, she sits beside me. "Were you up all night?"

"Orientation didn't finish until just before you texted."

She slurps the last of her coffee. "I'm glad I caught you before you went to bed. Thanks for coming up." Grabbing both empty cups, she sets them in the sink and fills them with water. "I need to get ready for work. Sleep well."

February 22, 2020
Maggie

I'm in the ER, dressed only in a tank top, underwear and fuzzy pink bunny slippers. I haven't owned bunny slippers since I was five. The dim red lights cast a bloody pall over the gurneys that crowd the hallway. I slog through the sea of patients, trying to find Rama. From under a sheet, a hand emerges and reaches for me. I back away, bumping into the bed behind me. The occupant rolls against me and coughs uncontrollably, wheezing in shallow gasps of air. "Maggie," Rama calls from further down the corridor. "Why aren't you dressed? I need help."

My body jerks. My heart pounds in my chest, in my ears. I open my eyes to a dark room. My bedroom. My bed. I was dreaming. Sitting up, I try to shake off the feeling of impending doom it left with me. I check my phone for the time. Six-fifteen. It's Saturday. I didn't want to wake up this early, but I don't think I can go back to sleep. After washing my face, I feel more awake. I text Rix.

> Are you still up? I'm having an early breakfast. Wouldn't mind your company.

By the time the coffee is brewing, my phone buzzes. At his response—

> Be right there

—my tight gut begins to relax.

Grabbing a second cup, I set it beside mine. The basement door swings open. I look over my shoulder to find Rix stopped in the shadows of the doorway, nearly invisible with his dark clothing and ashen skin. Is he a goth? Or maybe he's anemic. I don't know him well enough to pry. It makes me worry he may have inadequate health care coverage to see a doctor. I smile. "Good morning. Coffee?"

He steps into the room—into the light—and returns my smile. "Good morning. Coffee sounds good, but no rush." As I butter my bagel, he sits on the far side of the counter and gazes at me. "It's Saturday. You're up early."

"I woke up." After pouring the coffee, I set the mugs on the countertop along with my toast. My smile fades. "Uneasy dream. Are you sure you don't want something to eat?"

"I'm sure, but thanks." He sips his coffee. "Mmm. This is always so good."

I return his smile. "Thanks for joining me."

"What did you dream?" he asks. Frowning, I focus on my bagel, take a bite, chew and swallow it. When I look up, he's contemplating me, his face filled with gentle curiosity. "You don't have to remember it, but sometimes it helps ease my anxiety when I do."

Is it that obvious? "I was at the ER, wearing bunny slippers, and it was filled with lots of really sick people." I grunt. "And I felt helpless, like I didn't know what to do."

"Bunny slippers?" For a brief moment, his eyes smile even though his mouth does not. "Dreams like these are not unusual for people who work in places like ERs"—a crease knits his brow—"or on battlefields. The uncertainty of this new virus probably adds to your worry, whether you think about it consciously or not."

"Well, China did report the director of one of the Wuhan hospitals and a respiratory doctor both died this week. The conditions in their hospitals are atrocious. They don't have enough PPE, let alone beds. The nurses are working in diapers so they don't need new PPE, like they would if they went to the bathroom. They can't afford to put on new masks and gloves."

"Those are ICU nurses. They always take the brunt of situations like that." He gives me a weak smile. "Hopefully, we're better prepared here." His hand slides across the countertop, fingers lifting toward me, before retracting like the neck of a clam into the sand. The quivering of his knee causes a vibration that reaches clear to me. Surreptitiously watching me, he picks up his cup, sets it back down, puts both hands in his lap. The tremors stop. "What's on your agenda today?"

I smile at his shyness. "The usual: laundry; cleaning; a little yard work. What about you?"

"I need to catch up on some sleep." He gets to his feet. "Then, I have some business to take care of this evening." His smile returns, warm and genuine. "Thanks for the coffee. And the chat." After setting his cup in the sink, he stops to lean on the island. "Try not to worry, Maggie. Have a good day."

February 28, 2020
Rix

Since I was up all night hunting and working, I sleep until four. After showering, I find I'm out of clean clothes. I pull on a pair of recently acquired second-hand sweat bottoms—I've been slowly expanding my wardrobe —and gather my sheets, towels and clothing. As I sort them into two relatively equal piles, I pull my phone bill from the pocket of my jeans and set it on the dryer before starting the first load. Footsteps on the front porch tell me Maggie's home. She comes straight down and stands in the doorway, brows raised, eyes wide.

"What's wrong, Maggie May?" Unfamiliar concern tinges my voice.

She comes to stand beside me. "This virus is about to blow up." Her voice shakes. "Someone in a Kirkland long-term care facility died today. At least one of the staff's sick." Resting her hands on the dryer, her fingers land on the bill. She peers at it curiously.

"We've discussed this. We knew it was coming." I put my hand on her shoulder and give her a little nudge. "Let's go talk." When she moves away, I slip the bill into my pocket.

In my room, she sits on the bed and crosses her legs. I glance at the chair but she pats the mattress. When I'm facing her, she takes a deep breath and exhales slowly. "I've been meaning to stock up, but work's kept me busy and ... it's already too late to go shopping."

"Life's that way." I pat her knee. "Don't panic. Even if certain items are temporarily out of stock, I'm sure there won't be long-term shortages."

"I hope not. It'll be interesting to see how people react."

"Well, you're probably right about missing the opportunity to prepare. People get a little crazy when they're scared. It won't take long for stores to run out of all the decongestants and cough drops."

"And rice and beans." As her eyes drift down my bare torso, she absently murmurs, "You really should eat more. And maybe get out in the sun." She points to my side. "What is that?"

The bill lies half in, half out of my pocket. "My phone bill."

"Why's it addressed to John R Smith?"

"It's my legal name." That *is* the truth.

A tiny frown creases her brow. "Doesn't suit you. Rix does, though. Where's that come from? The R?"

"I've been using it for years." I shrug. "Is Maggie your real name?"

"My mother wanted Magnolia, after her grandmother.

She called me that, and it's my official name. But Dad"—
she smiles radiantly—"always called me Maggie May. I
picked Maggie when I started pre-school, so I guess I was
three." For an instant, her warm fingers brush the back of
my hand. "Thanks."

"For what?"

"Drawing me into a warm, safe memory."

March 3, 2020
Rix

After a chaotic weekend of binge shopping, stores
are wiped out of rice, beans, chicken, milk, cough
syrup, sanitizer and wipes, medical masks, soap, toilet
paper, and tissues, to mention only some of the suddenly
empty shelves. And, not just in Seattle, but nationwide. It's
been all over the internet. People's reactions should
continue to be interesting. Panic is a hard thing to predict.
And it's never rational.

The evening sky still carries a bright amber glow,
making me squint as I enter Woodland Park. Ahead of me,
a crow alights on a picnic table. I stride past. He follows,
swooping around my head. After dropping a shiny piece
of plastic in front of me, he lands in the path. "Sorry. Not
tonight." When I slow only enough to pick up his gift, he
flaps up to join his family in the branches above. A
guttural rattle scolds me as I proceed deeper into the
woods.

A runner wheezes his way up the trail. Moving into his

path, I smile. "Can you help me?" When he stops, I continue toward him. "Is this how I get to the lake?"

"Yeah." His labored breathing continues. Turning his head, he points.

When I'm close enough, I catch a whiff of his breath. Is this what COVID-19 smells like? His cheek's so hot, my hand reflexively jerks away. I frown. "Are you all right?"

"Just need to finish my run. Thanks for your concern." He plods away. "Have a good night."

Maybe I shouldn't have touched him. I use one of my disinfecting wipes to wash my hand, then continue down toward the lake.

As I round the dog park, I spot a strolling couple. Couples are tough for a single vampire to manage. Turning to face me, they block the trail.

"Oh, it's him." Cleve's disappointed whisper is nearly swallowed by the mossy understory of the woods.

"Hello, Rix." Bryer smiles. "How's hunting?"

"Not sure yet. The guy I stopped seemed really sick."

"I hate that. They taste disgusting, especially if they're on DayQuil." She wrinkles her nose, baring her teeth. "Must be flu season. Good thing we don't usually get sick."

"This could be that new thing"—I shrug—"COVID-19. Did you hear about it?"

"Haven't really been paying attention."

"It started in China and is becoming a pandemic. Washington had a death over the weekend—the first in the nation. Mayor Durkin wants folks not to go out." I look from Bryer, whose expression is disdainful, to Cleve, who listens intently. "Some of the big tech companies are letting employees work from home. A partial lockdown starts tomorrow. That's why I'm out hunting tonight."

Cleve's brows rise. "That's not good."

"It'll be slim pickings for a while." Bryer takes Cleve's hand, then looks at me. "You should join us hunting."

That'll take all night. I need to feed and get to work. "Maybe another time."

"All right." A fiery glow touches her cheeks as she forces a smile. She really doesn't like when people don't agree with her. "This time." She tugs Cleve into motion. "Good hunting."

"Good hunting." I continue to the lake. A lot of folks are out tonight—one last time before tomorrow's lockdown, I guess. At the south end, near the golf course, I lurk in the shadows of the trees until a lone walker comes near. She's sick, too. I let her go. I didn't realize the disease is already this prevalent. My next victim's healthy, and larger than me, so I feed until I'm sated before releasing him. That should hold me for several days.

Back at Maggie's, I try not to touch anything until I thoroughly wash my hands. After stacking the clothing I wore for hunting in the corner of the closet, I take a shower. I don't want to bring the virus into the house. Looks like I'll be doing more bathing and laundry from now on.

3

HUNGRY

March 12, 2020
Rix

After another unsuccessful hunt, I work until nearly five. Taking advantage of the abruptly-later sunrises—due to the change to daylight savings time over the weekend—I head out to look for an early morning jogger. Although little rain has fallen recently and the daytime highs are a balmy fifty, overnight lows still drop to a brisk forty.

I lurk in the dawn shadows of the Aqua Theater for nearly half an hour until a lone jogger appears. He pushes into a sprint along the straight part of the trail leading up to my hiding spot, then slows to a walk, panting hard. I saunter out to intersect his approach. When I block his path, his feet stutter to a stop. He gapes at me, still breathing hard. Good. He's not sick.

"Nice morning for some exercise." I don't stop until

I'm very close. Two fingers on his cheek nudge him toward the passageway between the stadium and the small craft center. "There's something I'd like to show you over by the lake." Like all my victims, he willingly goes where I direct him.

When I send him on his way, I head to Maggie's feeling warm and comfortably full. Tugging off my shirt, I debate whether to spend the time to take a shower or only wash before crawling into bed, but of course, I *should* shower. We're in a pandemic, after all.

My phone vibrating with a text from Maggie interrupts my decision making.

> Are you still up?

> About to go to bed. What's up?

> Can you stay awake to chat for a few?

> Of course. Give me five.

I carefully wash my face, torso and arms, quickly brush my teeth, and run a hasty comb through my hair. Six minutes later, I scoot onto a stool facing Maggie.

She beams at me. "Thanks for coming up. How's work?"

"I haven't been laid off." I give her a little smile. "So that's good. What about you?"

"We'll start teleconferencing with most of our patients next week, on Mondays, Wednesdays and Fridays. I wanted to give you a heads up." She makes a little "moue. My mouth opens. The relief I feel at her words overwhelms me. I can't fill my lungs.

Leaning forward, she studies me intently. "What's wrong?"

With a tiny gasp, I say, "Um ..." It takes a lot of focus, but I'm able to draw in a normal breath, which unexpectedly eases my tension. "I'm just so relieved."

Her expression melts into a smile that radiates a warm, amber blush. "I didn't know you cared so much."

As much as I hate to admit it—don't want to let it happen—I do care. "I was worried." My face pinches. "I don't want to lose you." I don't want to lose someone I care about to another pandemic. The Spanish Flu wiped out more than half my family. "I'm just getting to know you." She sips her coffee, gazing steadily at me. I go on in a rush. "Maybe you should quit going into the ER, too." I smile awkwardly, trying to make it look hopeful.

After drifting away, her gaze returns to meet mine. "They need me." The glow in her cheeks fades. "Soon, they'll need me even more."

I can't maintain my forced smile. Her conviction echoes my mother's. I nod. "I'm sure they will."

The melted butter on her toasted bagel begins to solidify. She picks it up and peers at the surface, then takes a bite. I sip my coffee in the cumbrous silence. After shifting on her stool and setting down the half-eaten bagel, she looks up. Her smile returns. "In good-ish news, did you hear the WHO declared a pandemic? In response, Inslee banned gatherings of more than two hundred fifty."

"That should help." I nod encouragingly. "It'll at least prevent the Sounders from holding another match."

"They should never have done that." Her frown eases to a tiny grin. "In better news, Seattle restaurants are providing our meals at the hospital, so I don't need to worry about dinners on the nights I go to the ER."

"That's a generous thing to do."

"I think they're getting reimbursed for part of it through customer donations."

"People are thankful. Contributing to the meals is one way to express it." I shrug. "Lots of restaurants are struggling. It all works out."

"Well, it makes us feel appreciated." She looks at her phone. "Ugh. I need to go. Thanks for joining me." Slipping off her stool, she takes her plate and our cups to the sink.

I get to my feet and head to the top of the stairs. "Have a good day, Maggie."

"Rix." When I turn to face her, she takes a step closer. Her hand begins to rise before she notices and drops it to her side. "Please don't worry too much. I'm being as safe as I can, and we're taking lots of precautions at work."

"I'll try."

"Sleep well."

March 19, 2020
Rix

The thumps and bumps of Maggie moving around the house now frequently interrupt my sleep. I hadn't realized how normal the quiet had become for me until it was disturbed. Being hungry doesn't help. Hunting takes up more and more of my nights, with only occasional success. For the past four nights, I gave up to get back in time to work—I don't want to give them any reason to let me go—and that was after an unsuccessful hunt last Saturday.

The past few days have been lovely. This afternoon already reached sixty-one, warm for March in Seattle. I hope it draws out more folks at the park this evening. With daylight savings time in effect on top of the quickly lengthening days, I can't go out to hunt until nearly seven-thirty. I sleep while I wait.

At a quarter of five, Maggie texts.

> Are you up?

I debate answering. Working from home so much, she's been cooking for herself and asked several times if I'd join her for dinner. I can't have dinner with her. My best defense is to be asleep. Rolling over, I cover my head with my blanket to block out the daylight that leaks in around the blinds, and to muffle the sound of her movements upstairs.

A little after six, the thud of the front door closing awakens me. It's still light, but I get up. Maggie texted more messages while I slept.

> Going out for a run.

> Heading in to the ER. Probably home by one.

Although glad I won't be invited to dinner, I worry about her being exposed so frequently. Before COVID, she usually only filled in on weekends and holidays, but now often goes in during the week for half shifts. If I could eat with her—if I was human—maybe she wouldn't go in so often.

At seven-twenty, I wait by the door, fidgeting for three minutes with an overabundance of caution until the sun officially sets. I head to Woodland Park, feeling a little queasy. I need to find someone tonight.

The vacant streets are not encouraging, and neither are the empty paths leading past the Rose Garden and through the tunnel to the overpass that leads to Lower Woodland Park. As I cross the bridge, I stop to look down at the usually busy Highway 99, eerily quiet with a complete dearth of cars. In the bushes beside the highway, a rustle draws my attention—an unhoused person pitching a tent for the night. They have enough challenges maintaining their health without complications from blood loss. I keep going, on my way to Green Lake where I hope to find some joggers.

Near the dog park, I stop to rest, leaning against a huge bigleaf maple. Whispered voices draw my attention down the trail beyond the tree. As I squint into the shadows, two people come into view. Can I manage two?

"This sucks." Oh, it's Bryer. "I'm so hungry, I could feed on a pig."

"That'd be the day." Cleve scoffs.

"Let's try on the other side of the dogs."

I step into the path. "How're you two?"

"Rix"—Bryer slaps my shoulder—"how's the world treating you?"

"Not so well. I haven't fed in nearly a week."

"That's too long." Concern fills Cleve's voice. "Are you OK?"

"A little puny." I manage a faint smile. "I was resting here to see if someone might come to me."

"You know that never works." Bryer scrunches her face. "You're coming with us."

"I don't want to impose."

"If Bryer wants you to come"—Cleve chuckles—"you're coming." Putting his hand on my shoulder, he nudges me along.

With Cleve trailing close behind me, I follow Bryer along a side path that hugs the ridge above the lake. She gestures ahead of us. "I saw some people setting up tents on the hilltop."

When I halt, Cleve bumps into me with a grunt. "Bry," he softly calls, "hold on." He peers into my face. "What's wrong?"

Bryer moves in close on my other side. "What's going on?"

"Um." Frowning, I look from one to the other. "I'll hunt by myself."

Bryer puts her hand on my shoulder. "You're hunting with us."

I meet her gaze. "I don't prey on the homeless."

Her eyes skitter over my face. She furrows her brow, but her cheeks remain a cool aqua. Looking past me to Cleve, she murmurs, "He's right. We should leave them alone." Squeezing past us, she goes back the way we came.

Cleve shakes his head, smiling faintly. "No one tells her what to do."

March 22 to 23, 2020
Rix

Back from the hunt with an empty belly, I hop online to get to work, just in time for the Monday—in Mumbai—planning meeting. As usual, Nalini's lead, Rakesh, starts with a status review. His eyes and brow, above his masked nose and mouth, are pursed. The room hums with background whispers. "Please, pay attention." The group quiets. "Nalini, your report."

"Two of my devs"—her mask-muffled voice quavers—"are caring for sick family members." Two? She only has five. "Also, two of my American contractors are out sick. We missed our deadline on Friday. I'm trying to figure out how to get it done short-staffed this week, while keeping things running smoothly on the DevOps side. We need to adjust expectations."

Now, the room is silent. For an extremely long minute, Rakesh's eyes stare blankly. "All right." He turns to Jagat. "How's your team?"

"I'm down a dev, and one in DevOps. We hit our goal last week, but just barely." He shakes his head.

The other leads relate similar stories.

"With the government putting the country into lockdown tomorrow," Rakesh says, "we'll focus today on prepping everyone for remote access. If you don't have a laptop or reliable internet at home, your leads can help you get things sorted out. We don't expect much progress this week, so don't let that worry you.

It'll be a week of learning how to adjust to our new work environment. Let's hope this can keep us all safe."

My Zoom feed stops. I click a text notification from Nalini.

> Work on any existing tickets today. Unfortunately, for the rest of the week we'll be on a skeleton crew for DevOps. I have you slated for Thursday and Friday.

> Do what you need to do. Let me know if an emergency comes up.

> Thanks for offering. Hopefully, by next week, things will settle into more normalcy, and we can re-evaluate. Don't you go getting sick. We hear Seattle is a hotspot.

> We were the first area to get hit in North America, so things were pretty chaotic, but we've got a good Governor who put us into lockdown almost immediately.

> That's good to hear. I need to go now.

> Stay safe.

> You too.

With few changes deployed after the meeting, the number of open tickets drops to zero. At four, I log out. I find myself singing along with the music playing in the background—Styx's 'The Best of Times.' People *are* hiding inside. If this ever was paradise, it will definitely be different moving forward. The front door opens and closes. Is Maggie just getting home? I text her.

> Is that you?

> Didn't mean to wake you. The shift lasted longer than anticipated.

> I wasn't asleep yet.

> I'm having something to eat after I shower. Join me?

> Going to bed soon.

I'm not certain I want to spend time with her until after I feed again, but I would like to see her.

> But I'll sit with you for a while.

> See you in fifteen. :-)

While I wait, I put on my last clean shirt—I need to do laundry, again—brush my teeth and comb my hair, fussing with a tuft that insists on poking up. I give up and head to the kitchen. Maggie stands at the counter, dressed in sweats and an old tee, with a towel around her shoulders that she uses to daub at her thick hair. "It takes so long for this to dry." She pulls a muffin from the microwave and pours a glass of milk before joining me at the island. "Are you sure you don't want anything?"

"I'm good." I study her. "You look tired."

"Exhausted." She nibbles her muffin. "And this is just the beginning. Welcome to the Age of COVID-19."

"When will you sleep? Don't you have patients this morning?"

"Two rescheduled, and I moved the other one until later in the day." She gives me a faint smile. "Thanks for your concern."

"India's going into a nationwide lockdown tomorrow. I wonder if that'll happen here."

"Hmph." She smirks. "Not during an election year."

"Especially with this President. At least Governor Inslee issued a stay at home mandate. He's up for election, too."

"I hope it works. And that he gets re-elected."

"He doesn't seem to have much competition."

"Well, there's that, but you can never be certain." After setting down her muffin, she takes a sip of coffee. "Even with good local government, New York City's turning into a disaster. The ICUs are overwhelmed, they ran out of PPE, and they're telling people to just stay home when they get sick. A replay of Wuhan."

"I hope it doesn't come to that here."

"We nearly ran out of hand sanitizer. You can't buy that, either." She yawns. "Our pharmacy began making it for us."

My hand finds its way across the countertop to bump against hers. I wait for her to look up. "Have you reconsidered going in to the ER? You're already working full-time with your regular patients."

"I can't not go." Her sleepy eyes fill with tears. "Don't ask me that again." She drops her voice to a whisper. "Please. You may talk me out of it."

March 26, 2020
Rix

The warm-down music of Maggie's yoga video begins to play. It's not loud or disturbing me, but this is an old house and my vampire ears are hypersensitive. Sometimes that can be a benefit. After waiting a couple of minutes, I text her.

> You busy?

> Just finishing my yoga class. What's up?

> I read about something I'd like to share with you.

> If you don't mind my sweaty body, come on up. The door's unlocked. I'm in the living room.

From the entryway, I peek around the doorjamb. With her eyes closed and her long curls loose around her exercise-flushed face, Maggie lies on her back on a bright teal mat, slowly breathing in and out. Calm and relaxed. I'm always so distracted by her eyes that I've never noticed how very beautiful she is. The soft curve of her jaw; the smooth arch of her brows; full lips turned up in a slight smile. I want to speak, to let her know I'm here. My lungs fail to fill. I should go, but my gaze lingers. I tear my eyes away. Spin. Trip over a wayward shoe.

"Rix?" Her voice holds concern. I gasp and look

through the doorway. She's sitting cross-legged in the middle of the mat. A soft amber glow tells me she's serene, curious, full of trust and affection.

"Sorry to startle you," I sputter. "There was a shoe."

"I should've listened to Dad about putting my things away." Her cheeks ignite in a ruby burst, which quickly fades. "Come on in." She pats the rug. "I'd invite you to join me, but the mat's all sweaty, too." When she grins, her dark eyes gleam like Tahitian pearls. "What did you want to tell me?"

"Um." I blink. It's not quite time. What else did I read? "Um." I drop to sitting where she indicated and try to return her smile. She studies me, bemused. Taking a deep breath, I blurt, "Dr Fauci didn't get fired today."

"That's what you wanted to tell me?" She giggles. "I mean, it's important, and not a given, but—" A bang outside grabs her attention, followed by honking horns. Her expression turns to concern. "What's going on?"

"This is what I wanted to share with you." I hop to my feet and offer my hand. "Let's go out on the porch."

Outside, in the normally COVID-silent evening, from every porch and from every direction around us, people beat on pots and clang bells and hoot and holler. Wonder replaces her worry. "What is this?"

"It's your neighbors thanking you for doing your job." I'm really glad she's surprised. "Making a joyful noise."

"I didn't know they were doing that here." A couple of tears trickle down her glowing cheeks. "Thanks for making sure I didn't miss this." She takes my arm. I tense, but then relax as I watch her enjoy this magical moment. We stand in the cold spring night until the cacophony dwindles to random bangs beyond her street. "Thanks, Rix." Giving my arm a little squeeze, she releases it. "Let's go inside. I'm getting cold." I follow her through the door, shutting it behind me. In the entryway, her hungry gaze lingers on me. "I'm off tonight. Wait for me to shower." Her eyes tug at my will. "We could have dinner or something."

"That sounds very nice." I nearly give in, then croak, "But I need to work." I also need to feed.

"I wish our schedules synced up better." She touches my arm. "Thanks again. This was really special."

April 4, 2020
Rix

Just after midnight, I return, still hungry. The wind— on top of the pandemic—probably had something to do with the dearth of people. In the cold temperatures that went with it, my body cooled. Without the warmth a good feeding brings, I'm looking forward to a long, hot shower. As I take off my shoes, Maggie arrives home. Even though it'll take a while for her to go through her decontamination ritual, I'll wait to shower until she's done. The last thing I want to do is keep her from her sleep.

I wash my hands while reciting the Bene Gesserit 'Litany Against Fear,' which I already knew by heart before its suggested use for washing adequately long in the Age of COVID-19. It's certainly preferable to singing

'Happy Birthday' twice. I sit on my bed and open my laptop. The videos of the nurses at Mt Sinai West Hospital in Manhattan, wearing garbage bags because there aren't enough gowns, still headline the news a week later. Joining those are reports on the lack of N95s, forcing nurses to re-use their masks, designed for use with a single patient, for an entire week. With overflowing morgues, hundreds of victims fill rows of freezer trailers. Will Seattle get to that point?

The other major headline is the CDC coming out for masking and stay-at-home orders, but the President saying it's voluntary. It's unconscionable—but not surprising, with the current Administration—that the United States finds itself in such dire straits.

As a plethora of ads loads on the news sites, my computer heats up, warming my hands and thighs. My phone vibrates with a text from Maggie.

Awake?

I was hoping she'd text before she went to bed.

doomscrolling

Will you keep me company while I eat?

Anything for you. :-)

I quickly run a comb through my hair. By the time I arrive, she's pulling out a microwave meal. Sitting across from her as she carefully peels off the plastic, I study her. "You look tired." Glancing up with puffy, red eyes, she nods, stirs her food and takes a cautious bite. I lean toward her. "Are you OK?" When she only takes another bite, I reach my hand to the center of the island. "What's wrong, Maggie May?"

Letting her hand fall to the countertop, she drops her head and squeezes her eyes shut. She swallows hard, choking down her mouthful of food, and takes a quick sip of water.

"Maggie?" I slide off my stool to lean even closer.

"I'm all right." Her soft voice cracks. She looks up at me. "It was a rough night."

"Do you want to share about it?"

Nodding, she stands. "Can we talk in the living room?"

I follow and sit next to her on the couch, where she's right in the middle. I guess she needs me to be close to her. When she scoots nearer—so our thighs touch—the contact makes me stiffen. I try to relax. "What happened?"

"She died." Barely more than a whisper.

"Who died?" I watch as she worries her lower lip between her teeth. "You sure you want to talk about this?"

She nods again, then peers at me. "Will you hold me?"

My brows shoot up. I did not expect this or would definitely have taken a shower. "Um ..."

"Please?"

I melt into the warmth of her dark eyes. "OK." My voice is half a pitch too high. I raise my arm and drape it over her shoulder as she snugs in against me. "How's that?" My hand hangs awkwardly in the air beyond her.

She looks up at me. "Why are you so cold?"

"I went out for a walk ... um ... just before you got home." The words tumble out in a rush. "I didn't realize it was so cold out, and I was going to take a shower"—time to stop talking, Rix—"but you got home, and I waited for you to bathe, but then ..." I take a breath and slow myself. "But then, you asked me to come up."

A slight smile makes her cheeks glow. "That's all right. I'll warm you."

I can't help smiling in return. "Are you going to tell me?"

"About what? Oh." She inhales deeply, huffs it out. "Rama's aunt died tonight." She drops her head to my shoulder. I breathe her in. My hand relaxes, rests on her arm. She snuggles closer. "She was a nurse in New York City." Her voice rises with her indignation. "Did you know they're only issued one mask a week? And you can't buy them."

"I heard about that." I can't bear to tell her about the President's comments.

"I should have sent her some of Dad's masks. She got sick ten days ago, and now she's gone." Tears well in her eyes. "Rama couldn't go back to be with her. She died all alone. Like everyone in this damned pandemic." They spill down her cheeks. "I was there when he got the call. I sat with him, but couldn't touch him." With a shaking voice, she sobs, "He's my best friend, and I couldn't hold him."

As weeping wracks her body, I pull her closer, wrap my other arm around her. This feels ... exceptionally nice. I haven't held anyone with any affection in eighty years. My tears—for Rama; for his aunt; for Maggie; for myself —fall onto her hair. I let go to wipe at them.

Sniffing loudly, she draws away from me, in search of a

box of tissues. "Sorry." After handing me one, she daubs her eyes and blows her nose. "I thought I was done with that."

"Don't ever be sorry for how you feel."

"Thanks for being with me. This keeps getting harder and harder."

"Any time you need me, just let me know." I rub her back. "I'll be here for you. That's what friends are for."

Her smile returns, along with the radiance in her cheeks. "I should go to bed now."

"Sleep well, Maggie May."

April 6, 2020
Rix

Since I haven't had any luck hunting at Woodland Park, I head to Old Ballard. As I near Leary Avenue, the lovely early twentieth-century homes give way to restaurants, boutique breweries and a small private elementary school—all closed due to COVID—light industrial businesses and a power substation, with a smattering of post-World War Two houses interspersed among them. Decrepit motor homes, campers and cars, covered with blue tarps and surrounded with personal belongings, crowd both sides of the streets. Tents occupy every open public space. Under the Ballard Bridge, I walk in the street. The sidewalks are filled with folks who don't even have a tent, so lie in sleeping bags, or simply huddle on cardboard, wrapped in multicolored blankets handed out by overflowing shelters. Each one tempts me. I increase my pace.

As I turn down Ballard Avenue, which normally hosts a thriving nightlife, I see absolutely no one. The unhoused are obviously not welcome here. The hush is disquieting. I stop to look through the windows of the single business with any interior lights on, Canvas Supply Company, where several masked folks work the sewing machines. A sign in the window says they're not open to the public while they help fill the dearth of PPE by making masks and gowns for our medical professionals. I stand and watch for a long time, until my hunger drives me on.

Nearly all of the remaining shops and restaurants that line the street—most of them shut down, at least temporarily—have covered their windows with plywood, painted with brightly colored murals. Many include inspirational messages like *Stay strong* and *This too shall pass*. The fantastical beasts enchant me—a smiling bear, a joyful elephant, a purple tiger and crow, a blue dog, and even a Bigfoot. I spend far too long stopping at each one. I've never seen anything like it.

When I get to the main drag, Market Street, I turn left. No people. No cars. Nothing is open. Many of these businesses have also covered their windows with plywood. Even though I doubt I'll find anyone, I walk all the way down the commercial street, past older two-story brick buildings being rapidly replaced by modern ones—all concrete and glass—to the Locks, as the locals call it. Or the Ballard Locks, if a tourist is looking for it. Or, officially, the Hiram M Chittenden Locks and Carl S English Jr

Botanical Garden. It's not even eight, but the gates are shut and locked. A sign says the park will be closed until further notice due to the lockdown. I guess there's no point in returning here.

I turn around and head back along Market through the main business district, along an older residential area, fast turning into condos, and up the hill to Upper Fremont. At the top, I turn right and follow Phinney past Lighthouse Roasters toward Maggie's street. I'm hungry, but I need to get to work.

Halfway down her block, one of the neighbors comes outside, unmasked, dressed for a run. Every exposed part of him glows faintly. My fangs extrude. I halt. He turns in my direction. Glad for once that I'm wearing a mask, I focus on making my feet move forward. As he approaches, I keep my eyes averted. Seeing me in my mask, he walks out into the street in a wide arc—properly distancing— and sheepishly says, "Hi."

It takes all my willpower to keep walking. I can't feed on the neighbors! After he's past me, he breaks into a trot. And then, he's gone.

By the time I rush into the basement, my fangs have receded and some of the tension leaves my chest. I don't know how I'll make it through this pandemic. The same way you made it through the last one, Rix—constantly hungry.

4

FEELING SAFE

April 7, 2020
Rix

The situation in Mumbai has gradually worsened, although their cases and deaths number nowhere near as high as Washington State, let alone the United States. Many of the full-time staff continue to be out sick or caring for sick relatives, and some have left the city to return to family in more rural areas—which will likely have the unintended consequence of spreading the virus more widely. This leaves contractor layoffs up in the air, but my contract expires at the end of the week. I'd like to be able to plan. Since many of the foreign DevOps contractors are out sick, I've had more than enough work. I'm absorbed in a ticket as Etta James quietly sings 'Piece of My Heart' from her Bumbershoot performance back in '80. When my phone vibrates, I jump.

The text I've been awaiting from Nalini arrives.

How are you doing?

Not sick, if that's what you're asking. ;-)
How are things in Mumbai?

Accelerating. We reached a thousand cases, and 64 deaths. Aren't things quite bad there?

Yes. In our state of 7.5 million, we're averaging 450 new cases and 20 deaths a day.

We also hear about New York City.

They're on a steep upward curve—at more than 700 deaths and nearly 10K new cases per day. It's really awful. Our state's lockdown seems to have paid off, especially here in the city, if not so much rurally. Each state and even each district has its own governance, so the rules differ—especially coast to coast. New York's more than 4500km from here. We may have reached our peak. And folks are asking to get back to normal. My guess is there will be more than one wave.

There's a pause as she reads it.

People are the same everywhere. My real reason for writing is to ask if you're up for another eight weeks?

If you'll have me. :-)

> Perfect. Paperwork forthcoming. Gotta go. TTYL

Etta moves on to 'I'd Rather Go Blind' as I dive back into the ticket. By the time I close it, my hours are up for the day. To expand my knowledge base, I browse the copious React tutorials. The packaged options are numerous, so I pick one that appears among the most marketable—ReactJS with TypeScript. The TypeScript is there to tame the Wild West flavor of the JavaScript language by adding typing, among other ways to rein in the language for folks migrating from typed languages like C. By the time dawn's peachy light leaks in around the blinds, the 'hello world' page is up. Such a change from the early days of coding.

When I hear the scuff of Maggie's slippers, I text.

> Good morning.

> Morning. Coffee?

> BRT

I position a stool so I'm not facing the window—already too bright out for my taste—and slip onto it. She hands me a steaming mug and sits across from me.

"Did you sleep all right?" I reach my hand to the center of the counter. "You look tired."

Stifling a yawn, she brings her shoulders up in a little stretch. "Just getting caught up."

"The new case numbers are starting to drop." I try to sound hopeful. "That's a good sign."

"It'll give us a little reprieve." She shrugs and nibbles on a croissant. "But people already want to send their kids back to school and eat out again." Her fingers brush the top of my hand. "Thanks for your concern."

"The rest of the country's just getting started. New York City hit another high yesterday." I should have steered this conversation elsewhere, but that would lead into the President's handling of the crisis, and that's no better.

"I heard they passed five thousand deaths."

"I'm so glad we're not there."

Her tear-brimmed eyes wander around the room. She blinks away the wetness. "Me, too," she whispers. She takes a sip of coffee and another bite of croissant. "At least, we have enough PPE"—words as bitter as the coffee she sips—"for now. We'll see how long they last. We started wearing them constantly." She attempts a weary smile. "A local company spent time developing and 3D printing face masks, too. They should give us a little more protection."

"That's good." I nod encouragingly. "That's progress."

Swigging down the last swallow, she slides off her stool. "I'd better get going. Trying to get caught up from all the appointments I postponed."

April 8 to 9, 2020
Rix

The local news is optimistic about the drop in COVID numbers. It appears the Seattle lockdown paid off, and the city may have moved beyond the peak. People emerging from their homes make me hopeful about hunting tonight, although, that'll likely increase Maggie's workload again. At the Woodland Park picnic area, I run into Bryer and Cleve.

"Come with us." Bryer takes my arm as she passes me. "We're heading down to Gas Works."

Cleve falls in step on my other side. "Gotta maintain our territory."

"I didn't know that's part of your territory."

"*Our* territory." Bryer corrects. "Have you hunted there before?"

I shake my head. "I've been down to Old Ballard and the Locks—that's all closed now—but otherwise, not much beyond Woodland Park in the north end."

"It's time you start carrying your weight. Since part of our group moved up to Shoreline, we haven't been covering Gas Works enough. Don't want the Capitol Hill gang invading."

"There's more of us in Shoreline?"

"We'll take you up there sometime, but that's a two night trip."

Cleve throws his arm around my shoulders and pulls me close. "And the three of us would need to share a bed."

By the time I'm back in my room, the night is gone. Bryer and Cleve are the most trustworthy vampires I've encountered, and I actually kind of like them. While I understand my need for a support group with others of my kind, and my alliance with them will likely keep me safer, the amount of time and effort involved overwhelms me. And, in the midst of this pandemic, I'm more likely to fill my stomach while hunting alone. After stripping, I check my clothes over for wear, tears and blood stains before dropping them on the small stack of already-worn hunting clothing inside the closet. I need to do laundry. Yet again.

The hot shower soothes my body, but not my soul. I don't understand Cleve's attention toward me. I mean, he and Bryer seem very bonded. Is she really all right with him flirting so overtly with me? I'm not certain how that makes me feel. Or which bothers me more. The times in which I was raised were very black and white with respect to gender and sexuality. Everything's become much more fluid. Regardless, the only one I'm attracted to is Maggie. I'm even less certain about how *that* makes me feel.

With the shower significantly adding to the faint warmth from my half full belly, I rub my hair as dry as I can, brush my teeth and head toward my snug bed before the heat leaves me.

As I plug in my phone, it buzzes with a text from Maggie.

You up?

My thumb hovers over the power button, but I open the phone.

Yes. You're up early.

Couldn't sleep. Have an early appointment, so I got up. Coffee?

I gaze longingly at my bed.

BRT

April 11, 2020
Rix

The April drizzle lets up and by evening, the temperature reaches sixty. After a quick, unsuccessful sweep of Woodland Park, I head out to the U-District. Young folks always hang out near The Ave late at night. Most of them are unhoused and surviving on their own—the most vulnerable of the homeless. I never touch them. I want to make certain no one else does.

At the Methodist church, where they hand out meals and provide a few precious beds—made much fewer by COVID distancing requirements—I scan the small gatherings of people scattered along the street waiting for food or shelter or a blanket. As I turn down the alleyway next to the church, laughter behind the rubbish containers draws my attention. Was that James' voice? Sidling along the big blue bin, I peek around the end. Three youths and someone deeper in the shadows pass a joint back and forth. The large turquoise-haired one spots me. "Wha'd'ya want?"

"I'm looking for James."

He steps into the faint light. "Rix?" Stumbling backwards, he searches for an escape, but there is none, except past me.

The youth turns his focus on him. "You know him?"

Keeping my eyes locked on James, I move forward into the tight space. The two smaller kids dash by, but the larger one stays put.

"I know him," James mutters.

I hasten my approach, grabbing him by the shirt and shoving him back against the church wall. The youth runs off. Will he return with reinforcements? "I told you to leave the kids alone."

"I ..." James cowers. "I'm so hungry."

"We're all hungry. Go back to the Hill," I bark, "and stay there. And leave those kids alone, too." With my nose nearly touching his, I whisper, "I'll be watching you." Letting go, I turn and stride away.

The youths peek from the darkness of an alcove. Their muted voices follow me down the alley.

"I wonder what that was about."

"He must be the boss or something."

"Where's that joint?"

I walk up The Ave, which is devoid of human life, although in the recesses, my vampire ears pick up the scraping and scratching of tiny rat claws. I'm so hungry, even the rodents tempt me. As I head back down

Roosevelt, the tightness in my shoulders and jaw relaxes. My dark mood turns to melancholy. I definitely empathize with James, but I wish I could get him to change tacks, and not stay the course toward the looming rocky reef. He'll likely take a lot of folks down with him, or leave a wake of dead bodies or worse—vampires—behind him.

I head west on Forty-fifth. At the Blue Moon Tavern, a young teen steps from the doorway. They all look more or less the same from behind, with their black hoodies pulled up over their green or purple hair. I slow my pace when another, much larger kid approaches. A shaggy mop of jet black hair, badly in need of a trim—everyone's hair needs trimming these days—and thick muscles under a too-tight hoodie identify this one as male. He grabs the elbow of the smaller one, a barely pubescent girl, spinning her toward him. Her fawn-skinned face is gaunt, but fierce. With dark brown tresses and a blue streak starting at her forehead, she might be considered pretty, if not for the snarl. The storefront shadows at Floating Bridge Brewing provide me minimal cover. Wearing dark colors is useful in situations like this. Neither youth spies me.

"Take your hands off me." She tries to shake her arm free, but his grip's too strong.

"Just come with me." His voice drips like honey. "I'll take care of you."

"No! I don't need your help," she hisses, as bold as my daughter was when a bully cornered her in the school-yard. "Let me go." Unable to break free, she kicks at his shins. He raises his other hand in a fist. She lifts her free arm to block the impending blow.

I step from the darkness. In a breath, I'm beside them. My voice is soft, but firm. "When a person says no, it means no." I said those same words to Eri's attacker.

His head spins toward me. "Where'd you come from?" Dropping her arm, he dashes down the alley.

I'm tempted to pursue him. He's a predator, after all. Instead, I turn to his victim, who openly gawks at me. She's just a child, no more than fourteen. "Are you all right?" I ask. "Did he hurt you?"

She rubs her arm and hitches her backpack up onto her shoulder. "I'm fine." The orange glow of fear in her face fades with the brute's footfalls. She's a little safer now.

For a brief moment, I catch a glimpse of my daughter's face, framed by dark curls fallen loose during the scuffle. That boy ran, like this one did. What if this was *her*, out on the streets alone? The image fades to reveal this dirty, gaunt child, evoking hazy images of the starving children at the camp. I push those painful memories back behind the tattered veils that shroud them. "Are you hungry? Dick's is still open. How about a burger and some fries?"

Her face brightens.

On the far side of Interstate 5, beyond the eerily COVID-quiet freeway—reminiscent of Seattle during a rare snowstorm—she looks up at me. "Thanks for that, back there. I shoulda been payin' closer attention."

"It's hard to do when you're struggling just to survive. You shouldn't need to deal with people like that." At a flash of fear in her cheeks, I soften my voice to dissipate my anger. "What are you doing out here alone?"

"Slowly starvin' to death." She shrugs. "Unless the virus gets me first."

"Can I help you find a shelter?"

"I don't do shelters. They just send ya back."

When we get to the parking lot, only one other customer is there, already ordering. We stand—properly distanced—on the blue masking tape X. "What do you want?"

"Cheeseburger. Fries." She flashes a winning smile. "And a strawberry shake? Please? They make 'em with real ice cream, y'know."

"I didn't know that." A sign in the window says, *Masks Required*. I pull mine from my pocket. "Do you have a mask?" When she only rolls her eyes, I point at the sidewalk, wishing I had an extra to give her. "You need to wait over there, then."

A few minutes later, I hand the bag to the hungry girl. As she shoves the fresh fries into her mouth—huffing and puffing to dissipate the heat—I follow her around the corner. After she sits on the curb, I squat and hand her the shake.

"I love strawberry." She draws on the straw, but frowns. "Still too thick for these stupid paper straws." Setting it aside, she removes the burger from its compostable wrapper.

Watching her eat gratifies me. I haven't made anyone this happy in a long time.

❧

April 16, 2020
Rix

Around midnight, after a few unfruitful hours of hunting, I give up and head for the park entrance. I haven't been this famished in a long time, and never when staying in the same house as a living, breathing person. Well, except during the previous pandemic, when I was very much a living boy. That winter of 1918 was brutal.

Near the picnic shelters, a lone runner comes into view. He slows when he sees me standing in the middle of the trail, and comes to a stop. As I step toward him, he gawks at me. I run my fingers down his neck. My thumb catches slightly on his mask, nudging his chin to the side. I'm so hungry, and the trees are so far away, and there's no one in this park anyway, I plunge right in. While I nurse at his neck, I glance beyond him to catch a glimpse of another runner, who changes course when she sees us. I stop suckling for a moment to peer after her. Could that have been Maggie? She should be asleep, or maybe at work. It couldn't be her. Could it?

Marginally sated, I let him go. "Stay safe."

"You, too." He trots off into the night.

Before I take two steps, Bryer—cheeks the smoldering coals of a dying campfire—appears like magic from behind me, with Cleve in tow. "That was stupid," she snarls. "What were you thinking?"

"Hello, Bryer."

"You'll get us all in trouble." When she's close enough, she shoves my shoulder. "I thought I could trust you."

"I'm sorry." I edge back, bumping into Cleve, but keep my eyes locked on the woman. "It *was* stupid. I won't let it happen again." Stepping so near her jacket brushes against mine, she glares at me. Cleve presses closer against my back, sandwiching me between them. I wait, body tensed to spring away, but I doubt I can evade these two.

As she shakes her head, the fire leaves her face. "You're lucky Cleve likes you." Cleve backs away. My shoulders relax. Bryer pats my cheek, not in a friendly way. "You're also one of the most reserved vampires I've met. Come on over to our place." It's not a request. When I frown, she snorts, "Oh, that's right. You need to work."

"I'm off tonight. Work's disrupted a lot since Mumbai's been in lockdown." I glance at Cleve. "Sure. I'll come over."

We exit via the gated parking lot entrance. Where I'd normally turn right, we go straight ahead a block before turning toward Aurora. At one of the last houses before the highway, we turn into the driveway.

"You have your own house?" I look from one to the other. As usual, they flank me.

"We just rent. It's supposed to be only me and Bry." Cleve crinkles his nose. "But usually three or four others are staying here."

Inside, a single lamp burns. Three couches line the small front room, leaving little space for anything else. It's tidy—probably because Bryer wants it that way.

"Home sweet hovel." She plops down at the end of a sofa, kicks off her shoes and tucks her feet up under her.

"Have a seat." She pats the cushion next to her. Isn't she finished chastising me? Leaving almost no room between us, Cleve sits on my other side. He slings his arm across the back of the couch and half-turns, with his knee pressed against my thigh. Bryer's gaze fixes on me. "How are things with your woman?"

"Fine."

"If I had a human"—Cleve smirks—"I'd never go hungry."

"I'd never feed on her," I say too loudly, then rein in my voice. "She's my ... um ..."

"Your what?" Bryer asks.

"My friend. She looks out for me."

"But you haven't told her, right?"

"No. And I don't intend to."

Cleve's bass draws my attention from Bryer. "She saw you tonight."

I purse my lips. "So it *was* her." This can't be good. How much did she see? Was it enough for her to figure out about me? About what I am? Do I need to secure new housing again?

"I don't know why you pursued a human," Bryer's voice drips with derision, and her cheeks glow an outraged goldenrod. "You can never be part of her world. You'll only hurt her when you're forced to leave."

"If you need a place," Cleve says in a gentle voice, "there's always room here."

"Wa-a-i-it a minute." Bryer draws the words out, slipping into an unexpected drawl. "He needs to regain our trust first." She pokes me with her toe. "How ya plannin' to do that?"

I study her. Her cheeks cool slightly to a soft maize. She's not finished scolding me yet. I try to look contrite. "All I can do is say, I'm sorry for my lack of discretion." When Cleve giggles, I shoot him a glance, then turn back to Bryer. "I'm sorry for not being more careful. I was hungry, but my behavior was inexcusable. I don't know what else to say."

The drawl disappears along with the heat in her cheeks. "We're all hungry"—she looks away—"especially since you pointed out we should be more considerate of who we choose to feed on." Returning her focus to me, she murmurs, "We all get sloppy sometimes."

April 18, 2020
Rix

I awaken to a bump. Maybe the front door? I stretch, remarkably relaxed after having just been roused by a noise. It's nice to wake up feeling safe. Don't get too used to it, Rix.

The gaps along the edges of the shades are blindingly bright. Stray beams reflect from the far wall. These days, the sun doesn't set until after eight, greatly restricting the time I can spend outside. With hunting as bad as it's been, I don't relish the even shorter nights that will soon be upon us during this summer of COVID.

My phone says five o'clock, but shows no text alerts. I was hoping to find one from Maggie. I haven't heard from her in two days—since that night at the park. Disappointment tugs at my dead vampire heart. That's how it feels, anyway. I text her.

> Are you home?

For a Saturday, she's really quiet—probably getting extra sleep before heading to the ER again tonight. I hope she's getting enough rest. Rolling away from the light, I cover my head with my blanket and go back to sleep.

Shuffled footsteps draw my eyes open. Light still leaks in around the blinds, but now holds a soft amber glow. The washer starts. I check my phone. Tightness grips my gut. She didn't reply. She *knows* I don't work on Saturdays. I open the text app and begin to type.

> Hey Maggie. Free tonight?

I delete the words. I'm not a predator. She can initiate the conversation—or not. What if she doesn't?

My eyes fill with tears. I close them, squeeze them, try to make it stop. Wetness runs into my ears. I don't want to lose her. With a muffled moan, I bury my face in my pillow. What am I doing? Vampires don't cry. *I* don't cry.

I haven't wept like this since ... since my mother died, what, eighty-five years ago? Not at the funeral, of course. In bed that night, after I thought my wife was asleep. She wasn't. She rolled away from me. Ashamed? Disgusted? I shake my head, shooing away the memory along with my tears. At least some of the tension has released from my chest.

Since I can't sleep, I decide to go hunting. When it's

dark enough and I'm about to head out, Maggie comes down to put her laundry in the dryer. I wait, not wanting to invade her privacy until she's ready. Besides, I don't want her to see me with tear-puffed eyes.

Even though it was a little cloudy today, the drought continues and the temperatures are balmy, still well over fifty when I get to the park. In normal times, lots of folks would be out. Not tonight. Or maybe I just don't notice them. I'm not trying very hard. When I get to the open meadows, a large fir along the fringe invites me to sit. In the uneven grass beneath it, I find a comfortable spot where I can use the trunk as a backrest.

The last of the daylight fades behind clouds as scattered as my thoughts. A shooting star blazes across the rapidly clearing sky. Out of the corner of my eye, a movement makes my head spin and my body tense to spring away.

"Pretty, isn't it?" Cleve drops to sitting beside me, throwing an arm around my shoulders. "You should pay more attention to who's sneaking up on you." He smiles his slight smile.

"Did you come looking for me?"

"Nah." Inhaling deeply, he impishly grins. "I just smelled a vampire. Why aren't you hunting?"

"There's no one out here. Where's Bryer?"

He looks up at the sky, points. "There's another one."

"The Lyrid meteor shower peaks about now. Where's Bryer?"

"Makes me feel insignificant." He brings his eyes to meet mine. "She's mad at me, so I came out for a walk."

I nod. "Me, too."

"Maggie's mad?"

I peer up at the sky. "She's not answering my texts."

"Bryer threw me out of our bedroom—*her* bedroom, I guess." He gives my shoulder a gentle squeeze. "I'm sure they'll both cool down sooner or later."

"Let's hope so or we'll be sleeping together in the park."

"That wouldn't be so bad," Cleve murmurs, lips caressing my cheek. There he goes, flirting again. He gets up and brushes off his pants, then offers me a hand. "Let's go hunting before everyone goes home."

April 23, 2020
Rix

Too hungry to sleep, I rise and dress. My last meal was the one I shared with Cleve, and neither of us was sated. Four days have passed since then. It's too early for joggers, so I poke at my little app that emerged from the React tutorial. A tool for vampires to find blood—not human blood, of course—and shared housing. Even if I spun it up on one of the free hosting platforms, it would be far too dangerous for anyone to use. I don't even back the code up on Git. But it fills the time until first light touches the sky to the east. It's barely past four. I doubt anyone will be out yet in this damp and blustery morning.

No longer able to sit still, I get up to pace my tiny room. "Come on, Rix," I mutter, "what's wrong with you?"

But I know what it is. I feel empty, like an abandoned house. Like I'm back in that horrible Nazi prison cell. Chained to a wall. Totally alone. I'm used to being alone. I *choose* to be alone. I'm good at it. This is different. I sit on the edge of the bed and cradle my head. "No more tears. Just get over it." I can't shake it.

Rising, I pace some more, like a caged tiger I remember seeing at a zoo when I was a small boy. At least in this room, I have light. I switch on the other lamp. As much light as I want. I turn on the overhead light. I can go out, if not whenever I please, whenever the sun is down. I didn't have that at Auschwitz. My cell was cold, the air dank. My stomach was empty—way more than it is now— for far too long. I sat in the near darkness with no idea what time of day it was, or even which day.

I check my phone. It's four-thirty-seven on the morning of April 23, 2020. It's Thursday. I know where I am. I know why I'm here. Maggie still hasn't texted.

Tugging on my hoodie, I stuff my feet into my shoes and head down the hallway. As I step into the garage, the door begins its slow, rumbling ascent. I stand, frozen, torn between retreating and seeing Maggie, even if she doesn't want to talk. I linger too long, transfixed by the headlamps.

She gets out, peers at me with a questioning expression.

"Hi," is all I can manage.

"Hi." She's not helping.

"Another all nighter? Are you getting enough sleep?"

Dark half-circles hang under her sad eyes. "We were busy. I'm tired. Talk to you some other time."

Scooting past her, I croak, "Sleep well," and then I'm out in the cool morning air.

By the time I reach the park, the sky's a pale pink-tinged grey. I only have about an hour to hunt and get back to my room before six. I'm seriously hungry. Along the trail leading to the dog park, I hear soft footfalls. I duck around a tree to wait. A lone man jogs slowly up the steep trail. I intercept him. He's not sick. Leading him behind my tree, I force myself to feed slowly and take only what I need—not what I want—to get me through until tomorrow night when work won't interfere with hunting. I let him go and head back to Maggie's before the sun can catch me, my hunger temporarily abated.

May 1, 2020
Rix

At three, Maggie arrives home. I text her.

> Will you be up for a while? Since it's the first, I'd like to pay my rent.

She surprises me by immediately answering.

> Need a shower, then I'll be in the kitchen for a snack.

> See you in a bit.

When her slippered feet scuff on the kitchen floor, I head upstairs and tap on the door.

"Come on in. It's open." At the counter, she butters a toasted bagel. "Just set it on the island."

"I haven't seen you in a couple of weeks." After laying the cash on the countertop, I wait until she sits on a stool on the other side. Her cheeks lack their usual warm glow, but maybe she's just tired. "You haven't been answering my texts. I've been worried. How are you?"

"Work keeps me busy," she says brusquely. A faint blush touches the corners of her cheekbones. She won't meet my eyes. "I've been spending more time with Rama. We're COVID buddies, so we're eating a lot of our meals together when we're not working." She glances at me with a knitted brow. "We should be wearing masks. You shouldn't even be in the same room with me. I have no idea who you see."

"I'm sorry." I shuffle back a few steps. "I'll wear one next time." When she doesn't add anything, I breathe in deeply, just to take in her scent, then step toward the door. "I guess"—I frown—"I'll be seeing you, then?"

Setting down the last quarter of her bagel, she slips off the stool and finally meets my eyes. Her rising hand stops me. "Rix, I saw you in the park one night ... with a man." She drops her hand before rushing on. "I know it's none of my business."

"Um. What did you see?"

She shrugs. "You two making out?" Her eyes drop to my chest "I thought you and I were beginning to be a thing, but I misinterpreted you." How am I supposed to respond to that? I take a deep breath, but my words won't start. I stand there for an eternity, with my lungs fully expanded and my jaw moving up and down. Her eyes drift slowly up to my face. "I'm sorry. I need to reorganize my feelings toward you."

"Maggie." My pent up breath forces the word out far too loud. "I ... I ..." I grimace. "You weren't wrong. I *do* have feelings for you, but I should never have let that happen." My eyes dance around her face, searing the image into my brain. "It's not possible for us to be together."

"Why not? I don't care if you're bi. I've been with women. But, I need to be in a monogamous relationship."

"Um ... that man ..." My hand covers my mouth, then sweeps off my chin. "I shouldn't tell you this."

"Tell me what? I thought we trusted each other. That you're my friend."

"I do trust you, but ..." My fingers flitter. "All right. I'm not what you think I am."

"What do you mean?"

I purse my lips. Swallow. Feel anxious. This is not how I feel—or rather not how I want to feel. I gave up feeling. It causes too much pain. "I can't tell you any more," I whisper.

"What are you hiding from me?" Her voice is soft and gentle. My eyes dart around, looking for something— anything—to focus on besides Maggie's gaze. They land on the floor between us. She takes a step closer. "Come on, Rix. Fess up."

"I'm afraid if I tell you more about me that I'll lose you." My gaze rises to her mouth. I long to kiss her. "I don't want that to happen. I've grown very fond of you."

"I promise," she says earnestly, "you won't lose me."

I look up—into those eyes. When she smiles, my resolve crumbles like a sandcastle enveloped by the tide. "I'm not a man."

She looks at me quizzically. "You transitioned?"

"No. At least, not in the way you're thinking. I'm ..." I can't keep my hands still. "Maggie, I'm not human."

Her brow furrows. "What's *that* supposed to mean?"

I squirm, press my lips tightly, but feel compelled to go on. How does she do this to me? I'm going to lose her. "That man at the park"—the words pulse from me, thick and salty, as if from a severed vein—"I was biting him to feed on his blood."

Maggie's face turns ashen, her breath reduced to shallow pants. She stares at me with the whites showing around her irises. "What are you saying?" Her whispered voice shakes.

"Vampires are real."

She blinks. Blinks again. Connecting the dots. Her mouth gapes. She gasps in a breath. "So that's why ..."

Tears blur my vision. I'm going to miss her so much, but Bryer was right. All I've done is hurt Maggie. I should never have gotten involved with a living person. "I'll go," I whisper with the last of my breath, and take a step back.

The movement startles her into motion, mimicking mine. Her dark eyes glisten with tears. "How could you *lie* to me?" she snarls, coals stoking on her neck. "I *trusted* you." My stomach clenches. I take another step toward the safety of the basement, my eyes locked on her face, unwilling to look away. I want to plead with her, to explain, to beg, but my lungs refuse to fill. "I let you live in my house." The volume and pitch of her voice rise, along with the fire in her cheeks. When I make it to the top of the stairs, she rushes to the door—"I want you out"—and slams it shut.

The click of the lock resounds in my ears, louder than any of her words.

End of Volume Two: Vampire Heart

ACKNOWLEDGMENTS

My heartfelt thanks goes out to all my people who encouraged and supported me while writing this work.

My mother, Mary, for her never-ending support of this endeavor.

My developmental editors, Coral Alejandra Moore (https://www.coralmoore.com/) and Morgan Wegner (https://www.morganwegner.com/).

My friend and colleague, Raven Oak, for helping with some of the nuances of self-publishing for the first time.

My cover artist, Jamie Noble Frier (https://theno bleartist.com/).

Seelye, Nicole, Keyan, Elly, Rebecca, Izzy, Ellen, Mitch, Sarah, Mallika, Em, Dan, and my entire writing community, including all the folks who've listened to me read and given me encouragement at Two Hour Transport and 2am Notes. Special shoutout to Seelye, Keyan, Nicole and Ellen, who read the four volumes that now make up books one and two, and gave me invaluable feedback.

My niece, Pam, for insider info on the state of her ER during the pandemic.

Fire Station #9 in my Fremont neighborhood for validating information on response times, including who arrives in what order, and for providing scenarios that fit the long wait for assistance (still only about eight or nine minutes, but they would normally arrive in three) in the scene where Rix first meets Maggie, in Chapter 2 of Volume I. This allowed my characters to have some interaction and bond. The Lieutenant at the firehouse asked, "Did he <the heart attack victim> survive?" Nearly everyone in Seattle does, indeed, survive because of the years of work to train and prep and provide funding for our MedicOne response teams to arrive so quickly and well-prepared.

Nisi Shawl and K Tempest Bradford of Writing The Other (https://writingtheother.com/) and Cascade Writer's Group (http://cascadewriters.com/) for scholarships to attend workshops when I was unable to afford them. DreamFoundry (https://dreamfoundry.org/) for providing me access to workshops.

What the Fuck Just Happened Today (https://whatthe fuckjusthappenedtoday.com/) for copious notes on political events. Donations are accepted here: https://whatthefuckjusthappenedtoday.com/membership/.

Wikipedia (https://en.wikipedia.org/wiki/Main_Page) and its contributors for numerous citations. You can donate to them here: https://wikimediafoundation.org/support/.

AUTHOR'S NOTE

Rix is a manifestation of my anxiety triggered by the Sars-CoV-2 (COVID-19) pandemic in the opening months of 2020. Like many, many other creative folks, I found I could not focus on my current work. I was writing another series of vampire novels, and preparing a backstory novel for publication. I just couldn't. I did feel compelled to write, though, unlike so many of my writer friends. All I could manage were dystopian flash fiction pieces related to the pandemic. They depressed even me. Then one day, as they are wont to do, a vampire walked into a story. One flash became three. Expanding them into a short story became a rudimentary novella. Then I couldn't stop. Rix became the vehicle for me to document the events I was witnessing. And those didn't stop either. So one novella became a novel in two volumes, in a potential series of eight or more novels.

I had never written before in first person, present tense, but all my pandemic writings came out this way.

Rix relates what I observed: the empty store shelves; the violent summer of 2020 (for me, live-streamed on Twitter); huge communities of unhoused folks; boarded up windows on businesses; empty freeways. But I'm getting ahead of myself.

I included the Footnotes section after Volume Two in the ebook edition to help readers remember the specifics of the times this story documents, and to have access to content warnings, if they want to explore them before reading the story. The Footnotes are available on my website at https://www.ramonaridgewell.com/footnotes-being-a-vampire, for those print book readers, and anyone else, who are interested in following up with events cited in this work. It felt important to me to be accurate in my retelling of these times. We need to remember.

PUBLICATION HISTORY

"**Vampires Walk at Night,**" a short collection of scifaiku included in "Eccentric Orbits Volume 4: An Anthology Of Science Fiction Poetry," DimensionFold (2023).

"**Vampire Seasons,**" a short collection of scifaiku included in "Eccentric Orbits Volume 4: An Anthology Of Science Fiction Poetry," DimensionFold (2023).

"**Wildfires,**" a short collection of scifaiku included in "Eccentric Orbits Volume 5: An Anthology Of Science Fiction Poetry," DimensionFold (2024).

"**Containment,**" a speculative poem included in "Eccentric Orbits Volume 5: An Anthology Of Science Fiction Poetry," DimensionFold (2024).

An excerpt from this novel, "**Being a Vampire: Seattle Vampire Tales Book One,**" included in "Two Hour Transport Anthology 2," Fairwood Press (2024).

Co-editor, with NIB and Keyan Bowes, of "**Two Hour Transport Anthology 2,**" Fairwood Press (2024).

UPCOMING BOOKS

"**Strength of a Vampire**" continues Rix's story as he adjusts to sharing a room in a house of vampires while they all struggle to find enough to eat during the COVID lockdowns. Coming January 2025 from Intrepid Turtle Press.

Here's the first couple of paragraphs:

I stand on the landing, forehead pressed to the door. On the far side, Maggie's breath comes in ragged gasps.

"Dammit, Rix," she growls, thumping the door. I've never known her to be so angry, and feel awful for being the cause. Can she ever move past this? Her stomping feet fade away. Turning, I descend the stairs.

In my room—my former room—I slip my laptop into my backpack. The camping mat takes up a lot of the remaining space. I need to figure out a way to strap it to the outside, but no time tonight. I change into clean clothing, adding what I was wearing to a small pile on the closet floor. After tugging on a second t-shirt, I roll the rest into little cylinders, for a tighter fit with less wrinkles, and stack them like bricks, starting with a pair of jeans at the bottom, followed by my old hoodie, three t-shirts, and several pairs of underwear and socks. My toilet kit won't fit. When did I accumulate so much stuff? I fondle the tiny brown bottle of vanilla extract. It'll be expensive to replace, but I lay it on top of the toilet kit. My toothbrush, toothpaste and comb go loose into the pack. I force the zipper closed.

Ten minutes later, I'm outside, staring at a key too heavy to lift. I somehow manage to lock the door. Swallowing tears, I cross the backyard to the little fountain. Its burbling in the moss-covered hush calms me. I slip the reluctant key into the basin. It creeps slowly down, clinging to the rough granite, until it disappears beneath the ripples of the tiny cascade.

ABOUT THE AUTHOR

Besides writing dystopian flash fiction and epic vampire novels, Ramona Ridgewell (she/her) has had two poems published in the speculative poetry anthology, "Eccentric Orbits Volume 4: An Anthology Of Science Fiction Poetry (2023)," and two poems in "Eccentric Orbits 5: An Anthology of Science Fiction Poetry (2024)." She co-edited "Two Hour Transport Anthology: 2 (2024)," which contains an excerpt from this, her debut novel, "Being a Vampire: Seattle Vampire Tales Book One." Her days are spent tapping on a keyboard to create pretty software. She also seeks out adventures, near and far; lures melodies from her piano, guitar and vocal cords; and experiments with combinations of edible ingredients—recipes are just guidelines. Although no little furries currently share her home, crows from the neighborhood murder follow her on her walks and drop little gifts to gain her affection. A proud member of the Dreamcrashers, she thrives in the Two Hour Transport community where she is part of the management team.

She can be found at www.ramonaridgewell.com, or on Instagram @ramonaridgewellwrites.